THE WILD CRY OF LOVE

It was impossible for Valda to do what her step-father asked.

He was French and the idea of arranged marriage came naturally to him. But she was not and the thought of being wed to a man she did not love—did not even know—repulsed her.

"But Valda," her stepfather cautioned, "you have never chosen a gown without help. Do you really imagine that you are capable of choosing wisely the man to whom you will be married for the rest of your life?"

Valda would show him just how capable she was. She would run away—with the help of the gypsies camped on her stepfather's estate. She would choose a life of her own—a life of independence, adventure and love.

BARBARA CARTLAND

D0029756

Bantam Books by Barbara Cartland
Ask your bookseller for the books you have missed

Barbara Cartland
The Wild Cry of Love

BANTAM BOOKS · TORONTO · NEW YORK · LONDON

THE WILD CRY OF LOVE
A Bantam Book | August 1976

ISBN 0–553–02804–9

Published simultaneously in the United States and Canada.

Bantam Books are published by Bantam Books, Inc. Its trade-
mark, consisting of the words "Bantam Books" and the por-
trayal of a bantam, is registered in the United States Patent
Office and in other countries. Marca Registrada. Bantam
Books, Inc., 666 Fifth Avenue, New York, New York 10019.

PRINTED IN THE UNITED STATES OF AMERICA

Author's Note

When I visited the Camargue last year, in 1975, I I was entranced and captivated by its wild beauty. But I was distressed, as are so many other people, by the encroachment of the rice planters.

The Camargue grows eight hundred thousand hundredweight of rice annually, and this is increasing year by year.

There are those who predict the total disappearance of the Camargue in ten years, and this would be to lose something unique and very wonderful.

For the present the realm of unspoilt nature—the steppes, reedbeds, lakes, and pools, with their flamingos, little cygnets, *taureaux,* and white horses—still covers some 86,000 acres, or very nearly half the Camargue.

To me, as I have tried to convey in this novel, the magic and mystery of this exquisite wilderness is part of the soul of France.

Chapter One

1899

"You cannot mean it, *Beau-père!*" Valda exclaimed.

"I do mean it!" the Comte de Merlimont replied. "Your mother and I have talked it over very carefully, Valda, and it really is time we considered your marriage."

Valda made an exasperated little sound, then said firmly:

"I have no intention, *Beau-père,* of agreeing to an arranged marriage with a Frenchman I have never seen, who is not in the least interested in me. When I marry I intend to be in love!"

Valda faced her Stepfather as she spoke with a defiance which only succeeded in making her look even more attractive than usual.

She was an exceedingly lovely girl, so it was not surprising that both her mother and Stepfather were much concerned for her future.

Besides the fact that Valda had the deep red hair beloved of the Viennese, she had blue eyes which were typically English, and to frame them dark lashes which her father always averred were owed to some Irish ancestor.

One thing was quite certain, the Comte thought as he looked at her. She certainly did not look French, and, as he already knew, the Frenchmen who had seen her when they were in Paris had been fulsome in their compliments.

But as if nature had not been generous enough in endowing Valda with a beautiful face, a slim, graceful body, and an intelligent mind, she was also extremely wealthy.

Her father when he died had left a very large fortune to his only child, and the Comte, who was an extremely conscientious man, was not unnaturally worried about his Stepdaughter's future.

"You know as well as I do, Valda," he said, "that marriages in France are arranged."

"Then I will not accept a French husband!" Valda said sharply.

"And do not imagine that things are very different in England," the Comte continued, as if she had not spoken. "An English heiress like yourself is always married off to a distinguished aristocrat who is finding it difficult to keep up his Estates."

"Surely there must be some country in the world where love is considered important?" Valda asked.

There was something wistful in the question, and the Comte's eyes softened as he replied:

"Love is what everyone seeks, Valda. In most cases, men and women who enjoy the same tastes, share the same interests, find in their marriage a companionship which deepens into love."

"You fell in love with Mama," Valda pointed out.

"That is true," the Comte answered, "but she was a widow and not a girl of eighteen, who quite frankly is incapable of knowing her own mind."

"Why should you think that?" Valda asked, and now the defiance was back in her voice.

The Comte smiled.

"You have been brought up very strictly," he said, "and although you have travelled a certain amount, you have never done anything on your own."

"That is not my fault!" Valda retorted.

"I am not suggesting it is a fault," the Comte replied. "In fact I believe it to have been eminently sensible. But the fact remains that you have never chosen a gown without the help of your mother. You would have no idea of how to travel from here to Paris without a

Courier. Do you really imagine, therefore, that you are capable of choosing wisely the man to whom you will be married for the rest of your life?"

"If I leave the choice to you, how can you possibly know if we will be suited to each other when we are together?" Valda asked. "Suppose I conceived a violent hatred for him?"

"In which case I would obviously not make you marry him, however far the arrangements had proceeded," the Comte answered. "But I promise you, Valda, because I know you so well, and because I love you, I shall choose a man who has all the qualities that I think desirable in your husband."

"I cannot believe there are many paragons waiting about for me to fall into their arms!" Valda said sarcastically. "If they are so exceptional, why are they not married already?"

The Comte sighed.

"I am not going to pretend to you, Valda, because you are far too intelligent, that the nobleman whom I consider for you as a husband will not find your fortune a main attraction. At the same time, you are very lovely, and I think a man would have to be made of granite not to fall in love with you."

"And suppose ... he does ... not?" Valda asked in a very low voice.

She was thinking as she spoke that the average Frenchman had not only a wife but also a mistress.

Her mother and her Stepfather would have been horrified if they realised how much Valda knew of the intrigues and *affaires de coeur* of their friends and acquaintances.

But the servants and even her Governesses had always talked in front of children as if they were deaf, and because Valda was interested she carefully gave no indication, which might have made them suspicious, that she was listening to their gossip.

The Comte de Merlimont and his attractive English wife filled their house in Paris and their various Châteaux in France with the gay, sophisticated, brilliant personalities of the social world.

Valda, being still in the School-Room, was not allowed to mix with their guests except for an hour a day when she came down to the Salon at five o'clock.

It was when they were in London that she and her mother had tea together, English-style, but in France the ladies merely sat about chattering or working at their embroidery.

Having greeted Valda in a somewhat condescending manner, they would return to the spicy gossip that had amused them before her entrance.

Valda would listen and store away in her memory the various items that she overheard.

"*La Marquise* has a new *cher ami.* He is charming and very attentive, but *Madame* Boyer is livid! He was her property until *la Marquise* cast her eyes on him!"

"Have you heard that the Comte de Rougement came home unexpectedly the other night and was furious to find Pierre alone with his wife? One can hardly imagine the Comte as a jealous husband, but perhaps now he knows what other men have suffered where he himself is concerned."

"I saw Jacques last week. He was with that fascinating creature from the Folies-Bergères. They say he has set her up in style in the Rue St. Honoré, with a carriage and a pair of horses which are the envy of all Paris. He is lucky he can afford it!"

At first such information seemed meaningless, but gradually the stories fitted like the pieces of a jig-saw puzzle into a picture of society which was supplemented by some of the books Valda read.

They would not have been approved of by either her mother or her Governesses, but she found them in her Stepfather's Sitting-Room and took them up to her bed-room to read at night after her lights had been put out and she was supposed to be asleep.

She read about love and, as she grew older and it was time for her to enter the social world, she told herself it was love she would seek from a man.

Because she was extremely fond of her Stepfather and he and her mother were so happy together, it had never struck Valda that a time might come when he would suggest that she should marry, in the approved French fashion, a man chosen for her because they each had something to contribute to the union.

Now she thought that her large fortune would ensure that her Stepfather would look first among the Marquises of ancient families or perhaps someone like the Comte des Baux, whose antecedents went back far into the history of France.

It was living in Provence that had convinced Valda more than anything else that she must marry for love.

She had been excited and thrilled when she first learnt about the mighty Knights of Les Baux, who had fought in the Crusades and later became poets and Troubadours.

Their Royal alliances spread from the houses of Provence, Barcelona, Poland, Savoy, and England, and they claimed descent from Balthazar, King of the East.

Les Comtes des Baux were one of the most powerful noble families that Europe had ever seen, and whenever she could do so Valda would visit the ruins of Les Baux.

The ghosts which haunted the shattered ramparts were those of men who loved or hated violently and fought to the death.

Valda would think of the Knights riding out in their silver armour, plumes in their helmets, their pennants fluttering in the breeze.

At the Courts of Love, of which Les Baux was the most famous, it was from the poetry and songs of the Troubadours of Provence that lyric poetry sprang, and to Valda they expressed all that she wanted for herself.

"Romance! Love! Beauty!"

It was something she knew she would never find from a man who was interested in her only because she was rich and in whom she was supposed to be interested merely because he had a title.

She walked to the window to stand looking out over the exquisite view that lay before her.

Provence in the early Summer was even more lovely

than at any other time of the year, and from the Comte's Château which lay between Les Baux and Arles stretched rolling green plains interspersed with high, dark cypress trees, fields red with crimson poppies, and the distant horizon deepening to blue against the sun-lit sky.

"Will you not trust me, Valda, to do what is best for you?" her Stepfather asked, a beguiling note in his voice.

A handsome man, he had been noted for his love-affairs, which were usually of short duration, before he fell head-over-heels in love with the widow of Sir Edward Burke.

He had been visiting England and after they had been introduced at a dinner-party, it was doubtful if the Comte from that moment was aware that any other woman existed.

Lady Burke was lovely, but in a completely different manner from her daughter.

She was typically Dresden-china English, pink, white, and gold, with classical features and the sweetness which endeared her to everyone with whom she came in contact.

It was from her father that Valda had inherited her red hair and her fiery temperament; for Sir Edward had been an exceptional, and in some ways controversial, personality.

Now it was her father in Valda that made her say firmly:

"Whatever you may say, *Beau-père,* I will not be married off as if I were a package handed over the counter of a shop!"

"You intend to be an old maid?" the Comte asked sharply.

"Of course not!" Valda replied. "I want to marry eventually, but first I want to live a little."

"That is a dangerous philosophy for an unmarried girl," the Comte said severely.

Valda looked at him, then she laughed.

"I know exactly what is worrying you, *Beau-père,*" she said. "You and Mama are fussing over your one wee chick. You think I shall get into trouble like the de Villiers girl who ran away with a married man, or Hortense de Poinier, who set up her own Studio in Montmartre. But I promise you, I will do neither of those things!"

"Hortense de Poinier at least has quite considerable talent," the Comte said.

"Inferring I have none?" Valda flashed.

"I did not say so," he replied. "You have many talents, Valda, but they are not particularly salable ones. Not that there is any need, thank goodness, for you to earn your living; but if you had to, I assure you it is not as easy as it sounds!"

Valda walked across the Salon, moving with a grace that was notably lacking in some of her contemporaries.

"You are very plausible, *Beau-père,*" she said. "Whatever I say, it is like putting up a target for you to shoot down. At the same time, we still get back to the main bone of contention—that you wish to choose my husband for me and I have no intention of marrying anyone I do not choose myself!"

"Then I will tell you what I think we should do," the Comte said. "We must invite the young men we think most suitable here to meet you. You did in fact meet one of those we are considering when we were recently in Paris."

Valda thought for a moment.

"Can you possibly mean the Marquis d'Artigny?" she enquired.

There was a moment's silence, then the Comte said:

"I have mentioned him to your mother."

"But he is ghastly!" Valda exclaimed. "I danced with him and he sat next to me at dinner. I came to the conclusion he had never read a book and, though he was interested in horses, he knew rather less about them than any of your stable-boys!"

"You are very scathing!" the Comte remarked. "At the same time, he has magnificent Estates. His Château is one of the oldest in France and his name evokes the respect of every Frenchman."

He paused and said:

"Your position as the Marquise would socially be second only to the Bourbons themselves."

"I would just as soon be married to a flat-fish!" Valda said scornfully. "Indeed, a fish might be more interesting!"

The Comte sighed.

"Can you really make up your mind on such short acquaintance? Let me ask d'Artigny to stay. You can show him the beauties of Provence, introduce him to our friends, and see if he does not improve upon closer acquaintance."

Valda looked at her Stepfather and said quietly:

"You may think I am a fool, *Beau-père,* but I am not as foolish as that! If the Marquis comes to stay here, you know as well as I do we shall be so deeply involved with his family that it will be almost impossible for me to say that after all I do not like him."

"I think you will like him," the Comte suggested.

"Never! Never! Never!" Valda exclaimed. "And because I know you are intriguing to marry me to such a man, I swear if he comes here as a guest I will retire to bed ill, and nothing either you or Mama can say or do will make me rise!"

The Comte's lips tightened.

He was a very patient man but sometimes his Stepdaughter drove him hard.

"I have a feeling, Valda," he said after a moment, "that your father would have coped with you far better than I can."

Valda laughed.

"I expect Papa would have beaten me into submission," she said. "He was very hot-tempered, but you, dearest *Beau-père,* have always been very gentle and kind to me."

She moved closer to him as she spoke and lifting up her face kissed his cheek.

"You cannot change yourself overnight into a tyrant just because you think I ought to be married. Forget the Marquis d'Artigny and all the other eligible bachelors who have an eye on my money rather than on me! Someone will turn up sooner or later!"

The Comte put his arms round Valda and held her close.

"You are making things very difficult for me, my dear," he said. "I love you and, because I love you as if you were my own child, I have to do what I think is right. We will forget the Marquis d'Artigny. He is not the only young man in the world, but there are others amongst whom I am certain you will find someone to love."

"You are an incurable optimist, *Beau-père!*" Valda said lightly. "Let us go and look at the horses. They are so much more attractive than any young men I have met so far. What a pity I cannot marry a horse!"

The Comte laughed, then good-humouredly allowed her to lead him from the Château towards the well-appointed stables where he kept the horses with which both he and Valda spent a great deal of time.

When she went to bed that evening, Valda, instead of reading, as was usual, lay in her bed thinking.

She was well aware that her Stepfather must have reported their conversation to her mother and they both would be somewhat perturbed by her attitude.

At the same time, she was quite certain they intended to find her a husband and it would not be long before a marriage was suggested which would be to all intents and purposes a *fait accompli*.

It was inevitable, Valda thought now, that they should concern themselves with her matrimonial future after her success in Paris during the Winter.

It was usual amongst French families for a débutante to be quiet, unobtrusive, and very much over-shadowed by her elders and betters.

The girls of Valda's age were extremely shy, in most cases positively gauche, and were dragged round as a duty by their sparkling, sophisticated, *chic* Mamas without having any say in the matter.

Because besides being beautiful Valda had a distinct personality and was English, she stood out when she should have remained unnoticed.

She had plenty to say for herself and it was in fact impossible to ignore her.

Admittedly, it had been mostly married or elderly men who made a fuss of her, since the younger men were either firmly kept at the side of a possessive married woman or else were too nervous of the consequences of being seen paying attention to a débutante.

Nevertheless, Valda had been a definite success, and she was aware that many of the older women who were used to having everything their own way had made acid comments about her and suggested to her mother it was time she married.

"I always march my daughters up the aisle as soon as they leave the School-Room," one Dowager had said to the Comtesse de Merlimont. "The less they see of the world before they have their first baby, the better!"

Valda had not heard her mother's reply to this remark, but she made up her mind that she had no intention of having a baby almost before she was grown up.

'I want to see the world,' she had thought.

Now she remembered as she lay in the darkness of her beautifully furnished bed-room that she had always believed that growing up opened new gates and showed the way to new horizons.

It seemed that she was mistaken!

"If *Beau-père* has his way," she told herself, "I shall be married to a man who will have all the fun of spending my money while I sit at home and produce children."

Something rebellious rose within her at the thought, and she found herself thinking of all the countries she would like to visit, all the famous people she would like to meet.

Yet this would be impossible unless she was prepared to travel behind a traditional husband who would undoubtedly be as bored with her as she would be with him.

She thought of the elegant, sophisticated, beautiful women who graced the Ball-Rooms of Paris, and who seemed to glitter both with their beauty and with their conversation as brightly as the jewels that encircled their long white necks.

Valda could see their charm and she could understand why young men found them far more amusing and alluring than the débutantes with their demure white gowns, their lack of animation, and their shyness which made them tongue-tied and boring.

She had naturally never been allowed to visit the Folies-Bergères or the Casino de Paris, but she had seen the posters that decorated the hoardings. Posters which showed women kicking their legs high above their heads or looking provocatively over a bare shoulder.

It was all very different from the idea of a quiet family life, and a man who enjoyed such amusements would undoubtedly find her as dull as she found him.

"I will not do it!" Valda said aloud. "Whatever *Beau-père* and Mama may say, I will not be married off in such a manner!"

She found herself remembering how her Stepfather had said she was not even capable of choosing a gown for herself or of finding her own way to Paris.

It was true that she had been looked after, guarded, and directed by an army of Governesses, teachers, and servants ever since she could remember.

She was waited on from first thing in the morning until last thing at night, and certainly when they travelled it was like a Royal Progress.

"But that is not to say that I could not manage by myself!" Valda told herself defiantly.

She did not often think of her father: He had died on an expedition up the Andes when she was twelve, and before that he had been abroad so much that she had only seen him at fleeting intervals.

Now she thought he would perhaps despise the manner in which she had been cossetted and the way she had accepted tamely the lack of adventure in her life.

He had been an adventurer and an explorer—a man who must always be seeking the unobtainable. He had discovered ruins in Persia which had excited the archaeological world.

He had spent some years in India and made himself a huge fortune while he was there, besides acquiring a

unique knowledge of the various religions and hither-
to-unknown Temples.

He had visited Babylon and Samarkand. He had
reached China and had almost lost his life attempting to
enter Mecca in disguise.

When she thought about her father Valda could remember that always when she was with him there had
seemed to be a vitality about him that she had never
found with anyone else.

When he told her stories of his travels, she could
clearly visualise what he had seen and where he had
been because he made everything he described so vivid.

It was Lady Burke who had found life difficult while
her husband was away exploring the world.

She had every creature comfort, but she was the
type of woman who needed a man to lean on, and it
was impossible to lean on Edward Burke when he was
so seldom with her.

She had loved and admired him; but at the same
time, Valda thought now, it must have been loneliness
that had made her mother so eager and ready to marry
the Comte de Merlimont less than a year after Edward
Burke died.

Not that Valda had ever regretted it.

Beau-père, as she called her Stepfather in the
French manner, had been unfailingly kind to her, and
as he said himself, she might well have been his own
child for the affection he lavished on her.

Yet now she wanted her father as she had never
wanted him before. She felt sure that he would not expect her to submit tamely to a marriage that might be
a happy one, or might quite easily be disastrous.

Valda told herself she could never tolerate the con-
vention that her husband should attach himself to another woman or keep a mistress in some side-street of
Paris.

It might be the French way of life, but she was English. She wanted the companionship of her husband.
She wanted his love and she wanted him to be exclusively hers as she was prepared to be his.

Something idealistic within her shrank from the idea

of having *affaires de coeur* after marriage, as apparently all smart Frenchwomen did.

The intrigues, the subterfuges involved might be amusing to them, but to Valda they seemed sordid and very unlike the idealistic love she read about in the poems of the Troubadours, the Knights of Les Baux.

"I cannot do what *Beau-père* wants," she told herself firmly, and rising from her bed she walked to the window and pulled back the curtains to look out onto the night.

The sky was bright with stars and the country below the Château was dark and shadowy, yet very beautiful in the dim light.

'Somewhere,' Valda thought, 'there must be a man who will love me for myself, not for my money.'

For the first time in her life she hated the fortune which her father had left her.

Until now she had always imagined it was an asset to be safe and secure against fear of poverty or of having to live in a manner different from the way in which she had been brought up.

Now it seemed a disadvantage.

As she had said to her Stepfather, it was her money which her suitors would be thinking about, not her as a person.

If they considered her attractive that would be a bonus, but it would not really matter if she was plain and dull because her money would cover a multitude of short-comings.

"I cannot bear it . . . I cannot!" Valda said to the night.

And yet there seemed to be little alternative but to do as her Stepfather wanted.

Beneath his old-fashioned courtesy he had, she knew, a strong determination and a manner of getting his own way whatever the odds were against it.

He never lost his temper, he never stormed and raged as Valda remembered her father doing; but he was relentless and sooner or later the defences against him crumbled and without much apparent effort he was the winner.

"He will wear me down," Valda told herself. "The man he chooses for my husband will be brought to the house. I will be persuaded to talk to him and almost before I realise what is happening I shall be married!"

She felt herself shiver at the thought of the unknown eligible bachelor who began to loom as a menace, like an evil bird of prey, from whom he could not escape.

She moved from the window and lit the candles which stood on a table by her bed.

In Paris their house had electric light, but in Provence there were lamps and candles, which were somehow so much more appropriate to the ancient walls and the exquisite antique furnishings.

Having lit the candles, Valda sat down on her bed, trying to think.

"What can I do? How can I persuade *Beau-père?*"

Even as she spoke the words to herself she knew that she would fail to change his determined mind where she was concerned.

He genuinely thought he was doing what was right. He really did think that he would fail in his duty if he did not find her a husband, and those were arguments that Valda knew were unassailable.

She looked round her bed-room as if she were asking help from the objects that had been familiar to her ever since she had come to the Château Merlimont.

There was the beautiful painted furniture which seemed so fitting for a young girl, the pieces of Sèvres china that her mother had given her for Christmas or on her birthday.

There were pictures in their carved gilt frames which her Stepfather had allowed her to bring from other rooms in the house because she liked them and wanted them in what was her own sanctum.

On the Louis XIV sofa with its carved gilt frame there sat the doll she had been given as a child in England.

It had been dressed and re-dressed by various Nurses and by her mother, until it possessed an exquisite layette, every garment trimmed with real lace.

Beside the doll there was a box.

It was something Valda had bought for herself when she was in London last year and now it seemed to her that it was a key in her hand, opening a gate which might be the way to freedom!

The box was a Kodak camera.

When Valda had been in London, one of her English cousins had shown her a snapshot camera and had taken a picture of her.

Seeing the result, she had been astounded at how natural she appeared, and she persuaded him to let her use his camera to take some photographs of her mother, of the street, and of the carriages outside their house.

She had not been very successful at first; but then her Cousin George had taken her to the Royal Photographic Society and she had seen the snapshots of a man called Paul Martin, who, with a Facile, the first snapshot camera ever invented, had won the gold medal.

These were so natural and in a way so beautiful that Valda had become enthused by photography.

She had wanted to buy a Facile camera for a guinea, but her cousin had persuaded her to buy a Kodak, which had a flexible film marketed in rolls.

"The first daylight-loading film was made only eight years ago," George said, "and this is an improvement."

"How does the film work?" Valda asked.

"It is wound on a wooden cone inside a light-tight box and black cloth leaders are attached to each end of the film."

"And it is not complicated?"

"All you have to do is take one hundred exposures, then send the film to Kodak to be processed. It is much, much easier than trying to do it yourself!"

Valda could understand that.

The Kodak did not look very impressive and when she brought it back to France her Stepfather laughed at it.

But when he saw her first snapshots after they had

been processed, he was more impressed and even posed with one of his favourite horses.

At the same time, the camera weighed four pounds and was rather clumsy to carry, so Valda's enthusiasm gradually evaporated.

Often when she was out riding, the beauty of the countryside would make her long to take a picture of it. But it was impossible to carry the camera on horseback.

By the time she returned home it was too much trouble to arrange to drive back to the same place by carriage and photograph what she had admired.

Nevertheless, she had a black leather case with a handle made to hold her camera, and she told herself that sooner or later she would take good enough pictures of the peasants and places in Provence to show them in an Exhibition in Paris.

It was a daring idea which she had not mentioned to her mother or her Stepfather; but it was always there at the back of her mind and now she thought to herself that if she had such an achievement to her credit, her ideas about marriage might be considered more seriously.

It was then that she remembered that the gypsies would be camping on the Estate.

Every year at this time the gypsies passed on their way to Saintes Maries de la Mer, where on May twenty-fourth they celebrated the anniversary of their Saint Sara.

Because they were so colourful Valda had always been allowed to visit them with her Nurse or Governess when they camped in one of the Comte's fields.

She was fascinated by their painted caravans, their picturesque appearance, and their dark-haired, dark-eyed children.

All Provence was interested in the Festival of the Gypsies. At the same time, they were wary of the *Caraques,* as the gypsies were called.

The tenants on the Comte's Estate sometimes complained that they lost their poultry or that their animals were infected by the "evil eye" after the gypsies had passed.

But usually they were received good-humouredly and the young girls hurried to have their fortunes told, to buy love-charms and even potions by which they could attract the man of their choice.

"Tomorrow I will photograph the gypsies," Valda told herself. "They will make beautiful snapshots!"

She wished she could photograph the ceremony at Saintes Maries de la Mer. She had been told how the gypsy pilgrims slept all night in the crypt of the ancient Church, and how they believed great blessings came to them because they had made the pilgrimage.

'Those pictures would be original!' Valda thought, then suddenly she was very still.

An idea had come to her, an idea that was revolutionary and so extraordinary that for a moment she could hardly grasp it.

She sat staring at her camera; then she rose to her feet to walk once again to the window.

She looked out on the quiet silent beauty of the moonlit night.

"That is what I will do," she said aloud, "and because I am Papa's daughter I will not be afraid!"

It seemed to her as if for the moment there was no response to her words. Then somewhere far away in the distance she heard the hoot of an owl.

'They are mating,' she thought. 'And the owl is singing his love-song.'

She had listened to it often enough, for there were many owls round the Château, but now it seemed to have a significant message for her and her problem.

The owl was singing to his love! He was not forced to do so. He was free and the owl who replied was free too—free to respond or remain silent.

"That is what I want," Valda told herself. "To be wooed, to be pursued, but not for my money. If I do not fight for my freedom to choose my husband, my whole life from now on will be arranged for me!"

She gave a little sigh.

"If I make a mistake it will be my mistake, not someone else's," she told herself. "And whatever *Beaupère* may say, I know there is an instinct within me which will tell me if a man loves me for myself or for my money."

It was all a question of having courage, she thought, and being brave enough to break away from the softness of the life that imprisoned her!

She thought of her father exploring unknown lands, suffering discomfort and danger, even in the end to the point where he lost his life.

'It was the way Papa would have wished to die,' she thought. 'He would have hated to sit about doing nothing, just spending his money.'

Yet that was what they expected her to do because she was a girl.

Had she been a boy she could have followed in her father's footsteps and roamed the world; but because she was a girl she must be put in a gilded cage and the key would be kept by a stranger, this eligible young man who would be chosen for her by her Stepfather.

"How could I possibly be happy in such circumstances?" Valda asked.

Once again she heard the owls hooting, and now it seemed to her that they were nearer to each other.

She looked up at the stars.

Somewhere, she thought, they were shining on the man who would someday want her as she wanted him —the man who had been meant for her since the beginning of time.

"But if I wait here," Valda reasoned, "he will not find me until it is too late and I am already married to someone else. There will be no chance then of us belonging to each other except perhaps by some clandestine intrigue."

She felt herself shudder at the idea. It seemed unclean, unpleasant, to be thinking about love-affairs before one was even married.

And what did they mean anyway except a manner of passing the time? An escort to take one to parties? A man of whom other women would be jealous, a man who was like the cuckoo in somebody else's nest.

"I could not bear it! It is horrible!" Valda cried aloud to the night.

Then she thought of the camera and the gypsies in the fields beyond the wood. How often had she seen them there with their pretty, painted caravans!

Because they had interested her, she had read in some old books of her Stepfather's about the gypsies' wanderings ever since they had come from Asia.

They had been ill-treated, abused, and persecuted in every European country, because the people were afraid of them. They were thought of as heathen and outside the Christian faith. It was also believed they had magic powers.

And yet the pilgrimage to Saintes Maries de la Mer was Christian. The Church where they slept the night was sanctified and in the torch-light procession through the town they carried the images of Saints.

'I must see it for myself!' Valda thought.

The idea was gradually taking place in her mind.

If she went with the gypsies to Saintes Maries de la Mer it would be an effective answer to her Stepfather, who had said she could not find her way alone to Paris.

What was more, she would take photographs not only of the gypsies but also, because they passed through the Camargue to reach Saintes Maries de la Mer, of the wild horses, the beautiful white, long-tailed, long-maned Camargue horses which were famous in Provence.

Photographs of them, Valda knew, would be prized and admired by all those who talked about the horses almost as if they came from another planet.

Valda had of course seen Camargue horses which were tame: her Stepfather owned one. But she had never seen them wild, galloping over the flat, still steppes and sandy dunes.

"As beautiful," someone had once said to her, "as if they were ridden by the gods!"

"I will bring back snapshots of them," Valda told herself. "Then *Beau-père* will realise I am not just a pretty face, not just a girl who can be ordered into marriage without having a will of her own. I will show him that I am not only capable of looking after myself, but also of achieving something worthwhile."

She gave a little exclamation of excitement.

"Perhaps my snapshots could be exhibited in Paris. I might even win a gold medal with them!"

It was an exciting thought and Valda's eyes were shining as she looked up at the stars.

She felt they had inspired her.

"Thank you," she said with a smile on her lips.

Far away she heard two hoots following closely upon each other, and it seemed at that moment very significant.

Chapter Two

Valda slept very little during the night. She was planning what she should do and knew that every detail must be foolproof.

She remembered years ago, when she could not have been more than ten years of age, going into the study in her home and finding her father setting out piles of maps, binoculars, books, and implements on the floor.

He was holding a long list in his hand and as she looked at him in surprise he said with a smile:

"Come in, Valda, and help me."

"What are you doing, Papa?" she enquired.

"I'm making certain that my journey to Afghanistan is a success," he answered.

His daughter looked at him in surprise as he went on:

"It is detail that counts when one is exploring. Everything can go wrong and the whole project can be a failure if one does not think ahead."

He handed the list in his hand to Valda and said:

"You read out the items one by one, and I will check to see if I have them."

It had taken some hours to make sure that Sir Edward had everything he required, but Valda had not forgotten how particular he had been about the details of what she thought of as his "adventure."

"I must be as precise and sensible as Papa," she told herself.

She rose before it was six o'clock and dressed herself without ringing for her maid.

She put on a thin riding-habit because, even though

21

it was very early and the sun was not far up the sky, she knew it would be a very hot day.

In fact the weather was unprecedentedly warm for the time of year, and the farmers were talking of an early harvest.

When she was dressed Valda went down the back-stairs leading to the kitchen-quarters of the Château.

Already the under-servants were about, the house-maids in their mob-caps carrying dusters and brooms, the scullery-boys and the footmen busy in the pantry and the Dining-Room.

She avoided them as much as possible although one or two seemed surprised to see her and said respect-fully:

"Bonjour, M'mselle."

Valda walked down the flagged passages, passing the kitchens to enter the big, cool larders where the butter was made. Huge flat bowls of cream from yesterday's milking stood on marble-topped tables.

The larder was very cool and although the windows were shuttered to keep out the heat, Valda could see well enough to pick up a wicker basket from a num-ber which stood inside the door.

Holding it in one hand, she filled it with eggs and two huge pats of butter. Then passing through the first larder into another, she lifted down a fat cockerel, which had already been plucked, from where it hung from the ceiling amongst a dozen others.

Carrying the basket in one hand and the cockerel in the other, she walked out through the back door into the kitchen-yard.

There was only one old man there sweeping the ground. He looked up at her and touched his forelock.

"Bonjour, Pierre." Valda smiled and passing through the yard walked quickly towards the stables.

She was anxious to be on her way without her Step-father being aware she had left the Château.

They usually rode together in the morning after breakfast, and she knew she would have to find some explanation as to why this morning she had gone with-out him.

As soon as she reached the stables a groom came to ask her instructions and she ordered a horse for herself and said that one of the grooms was to accompany her.

It seemed to Valda, because she was impatient, that she had to wait a long time before the horses were saddled, but actually in little more than five minutes she had left the stable-yard and was galloping across the Park with the groom behind her carrying the basket and the cockerel.

Behind a copse of trees she found, as she had expected, the gypsy encampment.

All through May gypsies came and went from the Comte's land, being welcome to stay a day or so on their pilgrimage to Saintes Maries de la Mer, as they were on most of the other Estates round Arles and Les Baux.

Valda had always been fascinated by finding on the walls or fences the gypsy signs which they left for one another, giving information which was supposed to be known only to other gypsies.

Outside the Château Merlimont, if Valda searched diligently enough, she could find a circle with a spot in the middle of it. This she knew in gypsy language meant "very generous people and friendly to gypsies."

The circle without the spot, she had learnt, meant "generous people," while if there was a plus-sign on the fence, or two sticks crossed at the entrance to the field, it meant "here they give nothing."

Two lines crossing an upright one meant "beggers badly received."

The Comte, who had known the gypsies ever since he was a small boy, told Valda that there were many other signs which the gypsies left for one another in order to impart information which could prove lucrative.

"A gypsy woman of one tribe will go to a farm-house to sell clothes-pegs or baskets," he said. "She makes the owner's wife talk and she learns, because she is skilful, all about their family affairs, their hopes for a good marriage for their oldest child, or perhaps about the illness of another."

He saw that Valda was listening intently and he went on:

"When she leaves she will scratch some signs on a wall or mark with chalk or charcoal information which only other gypsies will understand."

"What happens then, *Beau-père?*" Valda had asked.

"Sometime later a second gypsy woman will arrive at the farm. She will tell the fortune of the farmer's wife, who will be utterly amazed at the intimate details she knows of their family life!"

Valda had laughed, but although she had visited the gypsies every year she had never allowed them to tell her fortune.

This morning in the camp she found over twenty caravans, most of them beautifully painted, and guessed that the Delgaddes to whom she had spoken for the last three years had returned again.

They were an important tribe of the *Kalderash*, and their *Vataf*, or Chief, a well-known and resplendent figure, was respected by many of the other gypsy tribes.

As Valda rode into the camp he appeared wearing his short jacket with its bright gold buttons and carrying in his hand his long staff with a silver head.

From his waistcoat pockets stretched a thick gold chain hung with pendants and on his head he wore a wide-brimmed hat.

"*Bonjour, Monsieur Vataf*," Valda said. "It is delightful to see you again. I hope you are well?"

"We are very pleased and grateful to be allowed to avail ourselves, *M'mselle*, of *Monsieur le Comte*'s hospitality," the gypsy said with the old-world courtesy which the younger gypsies did not have.

"I have brought gifts for the *Phuri Dai*," Valda said. "She is with you?"

The Chief inclined his head.

"She will be honoured to see you, *M'mselle*, but she has rheumatism in one of her legs and finds it difficult to walk."

"I will go to her caravan," Valda said quickly.

The groom had already dismounted and he held the bridle of her horse as she lithely slipped to the ground.

She took the basket and the cockerel from him, holding out the latter to the *Vataf.*

"With the compliments of the Château Merlimont!" she said with a smile.

He thanked her with a low bow, then led the way through the caravans, to where a little apart in the shadow of a tree there was one that was more gaily decorated and more attractive than the others.

This, Valda knew, was the caravan of the *Phuri Dai,* the female counterpart of the tribal Chief.

She was usually a very old woman, either the wife or the mother of the reigning *Vataf,* holding great power and influence over the women and children, and was always included in the Council of Elders.

She was usually called *Bibi,* which means Auntie, just as the old men of the tribe were addressed as *Kako,* a term of respect which also meant Uncle.

The *Phuri Dai* of the Delgaddes was sitting on the steps of her caravan and as Valda approached her face lit up in a smile.

She looked, Valda thought, very like a tribal Queen with her brilliantly coloured skirt, embroidered blouse, covered with a fringed shawl, while on her hair, which was still dark, there was a bright red handkerchief.

She wore an immense amount of jewellery because the *Kalderash,* being metal-workers, loved jewels.

Valda had noticed before that the arms of the women were weighed down with bracelets, and many of them wore anklets which tinkled as they moved. They all sported ear-rings, mostly of gold, but some were set with what appeared to be precious jewels.

The *Phuri Dai* greeted Valda, excused herself for not rising, and accepted the basket of eggs and butter with the graciousness and dignity of a Queen.

As soon as Valda had appeared, the gypsy women from the other caravans had all stopped whatever they were doing to stand staring at her with admiration and curiosity.

The children clustered round the horses, asking questions of the groom, but because she was talking to the *Phuri Dai* no-one attempted to come within ear-shot.

"You are going to Saintes Maries de la Mer?" Valda enquired.

"I think this will be my last pilgrimage," the *Phuri Dai* said. "I'm getting old, *M'mselle,* and we have come a long way."

"From Normandy," the *Vataf* explained.

"That is a long way!" Valda agreed.

"The young women wanted to pray at the Shrine and spend the night in the crypt," the *Vataf* explained. "They believe it will bring them good luck for the coming year and bless the children they have and those yet to come."

"It is too far for me," the *Phuri Dai* said plaintively.

"All women complain whatever they do," the *Vataf* said. "But I too wish to touch the garments of the Blessed Sara."

There were many different versions about the Saintes Maries de la Mer but Valda had heard the story from the Delgaddes.

There were two Saras, they told her, one of the Catholic Church and one of the gypsies. The first Sara was the servant of the three Marys—Mary Salome, Mary Jacobe, and Mary Magdelene, who came across the sea and landed at the village of Saintes Maries de la Mer.

This Sara, their servant, was not canonised and was buried in the crypt.

The other Sara, the *Kali,* was a Gitane who lived on the banks of the Rhône with her tribe and greeted the three Marys when they landed.

She was of noble birth and Chief of her tribe. *Kali* in gypsy language means "black woman" and she may have been of Egyptian origin or very dark-skinned.

Sara the *Kali* had a vision which told her that the Saints who had been present at the death of Jesus would arrive by boat.

When they came the boat nearly foundered. Sara threw her cloak on the waves and used it as a raft to help the Saints to land.

They baptised her and preached the Gospel amongst the *Rom* and the *Gadjé,* and Sara the *Kali* became the Black Virgin.

As time passed there was no doubt that the two Saras became merged in the gypsies' minds into one.

Thinking of Sara, Valda was silent for a moment, then as the *Phuri Dai* did not speak she said:

"I have a favour to ask of you."

"If it is within my power, it is yours, *M'mselle*," the *Vataf* replied.

"I have a friend," Valda said. "She is very anxious to reach Saintes Maries de la Mer, and as she wishes to take photographs of the gypsies, she would like to travel with you."

There was silence, then the *Vataf* enquired:

"She is a *Gadjé?*"

This was the word, Valda knew, for a non-gypsy.

"She is a *Gadjé*," she replied, "but someone who is very sympathetic and interested in the *Caraques*."

The *Vataf* looked at the *Phuri Dai* as if for guidance since a woman was concerned. It was her decision rather than his.

Quickly, before they could refuse, Valda said:

"Of course my friend wishes to pay for the privilege of travelling with you. She thought perhaps a sum of two hundred francs would be acceptable and a further fifty francs for every day she accepts your hospitality."

The expression on the *Vataf*'s face did not change, but Valda knew instantly that he was impressed.

Two hundred francs was a lot of money to the gypsies. It was a sum that would take them a long time to earn by working at their portable forge, as they were allowed to do by French law.

An edict of 1735 had declared that it was forbidden "to hawk tin- or copper-smith's work without qualification, or to take to their own place of residence pieces to be plated and repaired."

This, as Valda's Stepfather had told her, had prevented the gypsies settling as artisan smiths.

On the other hand, it offered them the opportunity of working, as they had always done, as itinerant tin-smiths, copper-smiths, and metal-platers.

Carrying with them a portable forge, the *Kalderash* moved about the country, their anvil only about eight inches long and three inches wide, with a goat's-skin used as a bellows. They managed with such primitive tools to mend and even make a large number of articles for domestic and agricultural use.

After Valda had mentioned the francs that her supposed friend was willing to pay, there was a long silence.

She knew that the gypsy Chief was calculating how many days they were likely to take on the journey to Saintes Maries de la Mer and whether the remuneration, large though it was, was worth the worry and perhaps the danger of having a *Gadjé* in the camp.

As if she could read his thoughts Valda said quickly:

"There will be no trouble, *Monsieur*—that I promise you."

"Your friend realises that she cannot enter the crypt while the gypsies are there?" the *Vataf* asked.

Valda remembered seeing in the newspaper that there had been trouble the previous year when some Press reporters had wished to be present at night.

Only the gypsies had the right to go inside the Church crypt, and Valda knew their vigil was surrounded with mystery.

"My friend understands," Valda answered. "She will not attempt to photograph anything that is forbidden and will ask your advice on everything she does."

"In which case, if it pleases you, *M'mselle,* we will take your friend with us," the *Phuri Dai* said. "She may not find it very comfortable, but she can have the caravan which belongs to my widowed daughter, who can sleep with me."

"My friend would not wish to inconvenience you in any way," Valda said hesitatingly.

Even as she spoke she thought how much she would prefer a caravan to herself rather than have to share one with a gypsy woman.

"Any friend of yours, *M'mselle,* is entitled to the best we can offer her," the *Vataf* said.

"Thank you," Valda said. "I am very grateful. She will be here with you at dawn. That will be, I think, about four o'clock tomorrow morning."

"We will leave before five," the *Vataf* said. "We have a long way to go and *Bibi* gets tired if we do not camp early in the day."

"This is the last year," the *Phuri Dai* said firmly. "The last year, unless by a miracle the Blessed Sara makes me young again!"

She laughed as if at a joke, but Valda said seriously:

"Perhaps a miracle will occur. It has been known before at Saintes Maries de la Mer!"

"It has indeed," the *Phuri Dai* agreed. "Two years ago one of my Grandsons was saved from drowning because he had the medallion round his neck that had touched the Blessed Sara!"

Valda knew that not only did they touch the Saint themselves, but the gypsies also carried miscellaneous objects with them on the pilgrimage representing those who were absent or sick.

Medallions, charms, and even pieces of linen and the clothes of a sick person would be taken to Saintes Maries de la Mer to be rubbed against the statue of the Black Virgin as they kissed the hem of her many gowns.

"Then this year we must hope for more miracles," Valda said.

She put out her hand and took the *Phuri Dai*'s bony fingers in hers.

"*Au revoir, Madame Bibi,*" she said, "and thank you for your kindness in accepting my friend."

She said good-bye to the *Vataf,* waved to the women who were still standing staring at her, was helped by the groom back onto her horse, and galloped quickly away.

She did not, however, return directly to the Château. Instead, she rode through the Park so that she would return from a different direction from the one in which she had gone.

Only as they neared the Château itself did she say to the groom:

"It would be best if you did not tell the others where we have been this morning. As you know, many of the staff in the Château are afraid of the gypsies and think they may harm them."

"That's true, *M'mselle*," the groom replied. "The house-maids at this time of the year will never go for a walk in the Park in case they should meet the gypsy men. They say there is a darkness in their eyes which is of the devil!"

Valda smiled.

Caraques, the name by which the gypsies were known to the people of Provence, meant "thief," but in the Middle Ages they had been known as *Rabouins,* and that word meant the devil himself!

Although the local people were supposed now to be very much more enlightened and educated than they had been, the fear of the gypsies had remained.

Although sometimes the local girls had their fortunes told, the older folk looked on them with suspicion and usually, when the gypsy caravans appeared, crossed themselves and prayed to the Saints for protection.

"In which case," Valda said to the groom, "I think our visit this morning must be a secret between us. It would be best not to mention it even to *Monsieur le Comte.*"

"You can trust me, *M'mselle.*"

The groom was a young man who had been employed at the Château ever since he was a child.

He was excellent with the horses and Valda knew he was devoted to her because she rode so well.

"Thank you," she said with a smile.

They arrived back at the Château and she entered the house by the back door, as she had left it.

When she appeared at breakfast, changed and wearing a pretty morning-gown, her Stepfather made no comment and Valda was aware that he did not know she had been riding.

She therefore did not enlighten him but merely talked about the plans for the day, finding with a sense of relief that he had an appointment in Arles and did not wish to go riding as was usual.

"Unfortunately, I shall not be back until after luncheon," he said.

"Must you go to the town on such a hot day?" Valda's mother enquired. "I thought we were to be on holiday while we were here and you would not have so many meetings and official engagements as you have in Paris."

"This is the exception," the Comte replied. "I have to see the Mayor about the disgraceful way in which the important buildings of the city are being allowed to fall into disrepair."

"I have been told they are a disgrace!" the Comtesse said in her soft voice.

"That is a mild word for what is happening," the Comte said. "There is a very early Romanesque Church falling into complete ruin since it was given to the Society for the Promotion of Athletic Sports."

"What a strange fate for a Church!" Valda exclaimed.

"Another, still earlier," the Comte went on, "is used as a Cabaret, and a fourteenth-century building where the Dominicans once worshipped is now a stable for the horses of the omnibuses that ply their trade between the railway-station and the town."

"It really is disgraceful!" the Comtesse exclaimed.

"That is what I think," the Comte agreed. "And that is why I have told the Mayor that something must be done. It will mean spending money, but the generations who come after us will want to visit Arles and not find it just a heap of ruins!"

"I am sure you are right, *Beau-père!*" Valda exclaimed. "There is so much history all round us in Provence, and it would be a tragedy if it was all lost and forgotten."

She was thinking as she spoke how fine Arles must have been in the days of the Troubadours, and earlier still in Roman times.

Already there was nothing left of the Courts of Love which had been situated at Les Baux, and if something was not done Arles would become just a modern French town and its glorious history would be forgotten.

When the Comte had left, driving in his smart Cabriolet with a coachman and footman wearing the

Merliment livery, their buttons embellished with the family crest, Valda smiled at her mother and said:

"What are you going to do today, Mama?"

They had both stood on the steps of the Château to wave good-bye to the Comte, and now they returned to the cool Hall with its marble floor and fine statues set in alcoves round the walls.

"I have rather a lot to do, darling," the Comtesse replied. "Can you amuse yourself until luncheon-time?"

"Indeed I can, Mama," Valda answered.

She knew as she went upstairs to her bed-room that she had hoped to be free, so her mother's occupation with household matters could not have been more opportune.

She had taken the first step in her plan and now she had to take the next.

In the attics of the Château there was stored a large number of things that could not be accommodated in the rooms they used.

The attics were large and lit from narrow windows beneath the dome which crowned the main part of the centre building.

Built over two hundred years ago, the Château was not only very beautiful to look at, but also contained treasures accumulated by the Comtes de Merliment all down the centuries.

Valda had learnt a great deal about the French furniture, besides French paintings, and she knew that many of the things in the Château were not only beautiful but priceless.

The Comte was justifiably proud of them and, as each piece had a history, he had told Valda the stories of how they had come into the family, so that each one had a special place in her affections.

In the attics there was a large number of chairs and tables which needed repairing.

These were kept here, Valda knew, until the craftsmen who toured France, visiting the great Châteaux to do repairs and renovations, came as far South as Provence.

'When they do arrive,' she thought to herself, 'they

will have to stay for months to finish all there is to be done!'

There were chairs with broken legs, carved and gilded, angels that had lost a wing or an arm, inlaid chests that required new hinges, frames that had lost a corner or some other part of their elaborate decoration.

But for the moment Valda was not concerned with any of these things. What she was seeking was a huge wardrobe that had been set at the far end of one attic, occupying an entire wall.

It had been built by local carpenters and was not a particularly beautiful piece of craftsmanship, but it was very useful.

In it, she knew, were stored the costumes that were used for the plays in which they all took part at Christmas.

It was traditional that Christmas at the Château de Merliment was very much a family affair.

As was usual with French families, the Comte housed at Christmas quite a number of relatives—aunts, cousins, nephews, besides his own son, daughter-in-law, and grandchildren, who lived in one of his Châteaux in another part of France.

The Comte had been married when he was a very young man and his wife had died when his son was born. His son, Phillippe, now thirty-two, had very little in common with Valda.

He too had married young, and had five children with his rather insignificant wife, who had however produced a large dowry in return for being allied with the distinguished de Merliments.

At Christmas Phillippe and his family, together with all the other relatives who were well enough to travel, converged on the Château de Merliment in Provence.

It would have been a rather boring three weeks, Valda often thought, if it had not been for Cousin Hugo.

He always insisted that they should enact a play, and that required so much hard work that the time passed quickly.

The first production which was performed before all those employed on the Estate was usually not only

amusing to the audience, but also great fun for the
participants.

The previous year Cousin Hugo had insisted they
perform Molière's *Mariage Forcé*.

When it had first been performed in 1664, Louis XIV
had appeared on stage dressed as a gypsy woman.

Female roles were then always played by men, but
the gypsy woman last Christmas had been in fact Valda, and she remembered that the costume she had worn
had been put away with the other clothes in the attic.

The key was fortunately in the door and when she
opened it it was to see a long array of theatrical costumes of every sort and description.

There were the long-sleeved robes that the ladies had
worn one year when they had enacted a play about the
Courts of Love.

Valda had loved the long thin pointed hats they had
worn, with the soft chiffon veils falling from them.

There was the silver armour which had graced the
men and she remembered how Charles, one of her Stepfather's nephews, had knelt at the feet of the famous
Queen Joanna and said:

"Give me your favour, gracious Lady, and I will be
your Knight—I pledge myself to fight the powers of
darkness and to destroy evil. Because of my reverence
for your Majesty, there is no mountain too high for
me to scale, no river too wide for me to cross. And if
God wills it, I am prepared to die to prove my love!"

Spoken in Charles's deep voice, it had given Valda a
little thrill as she listened.

'One day,' she thought, 'someone will love me
enough to speak to me in such a way.'

The history of Provence excited her. There were
Knights and villains, murder, treason, chivalry, and
jousting.

But above all else, love.

Cardinal Richelieu had ordered the destruction of
the great fortress of Les Baux because it was too strong
and too powerful. It took a month to destroy even with
the use of gunpowder.

But when Valda stood among its ruins and looked at the great grey cliffs, the silver ribbon of the Rhône, and the distinct blue haze of the Mediterranean, she knew its spirit had not died.

The splendour, chivalry, the beauty, and love still lived in the heart of Provence.

"And in mine!" she told herself.

In the wardrobe there were also the doublets and hose in which the actors had dressed themselves for a play that had as its heroine the beautiful Diane de Poitiers.

Her mother had played that part, and she had looked so beautiful with her fair hair and blue eyes that the Comte had declared in Valda's hearing that he had fallen in love with her all over again!

On the floor of the wardrobe was the Basque drum that as the gypsy woman Valda had carried in *Mariage Forcé*.

It was what most people called a tambourine and it had little bells which had accompanied her when she had danced on the stage so gracefully that the audience had applauded loudly and she had been forced to give an encore.

She was however at the moment not interested in the drum.

She was looking for the costume she had worn and she found it hung up between the robe of a Cardinal and an elaborate creation that might have been intended for Cleopatra.

It was almost identical to the clothes the gypsy women had been wearing this morning when she had visited the camp.

There was a red skirt over a large number of petticoats, a pretty embroidered blouse, low-necked and short-sleeved, and a black velvet bodice which was laced down the front.

Valda took them down and put them over her arm, and then searched for the red leather slippers with their silver buckles which she had worn with them.

She found them, and beside them neatly folded was

the red handkerchief which had covered her hair together with a pair of large circular golden ear-rings and a number of gold bracelets.

She picked them up, shut the wardrobe doors, and coming down from the attics looked anxiously up and down the corridor in case she should encounter her mother or the Housekeeper.

There was however no-one about and she gained her own room in safety.

She put the clothes in the bottom drawer of the painted chest, locked it, and took away the key.

It was not likely that one of the maids would investigate its contents, for as a rule there was little or nothing in it, but she did not wish to take any chances.

Now she had a dress to wear which would not make her conspicuous when she joined the gypsies, but she might wish to return home alone, in which case she would require some of her ordinary clothes with her as well.

The difficulty was how to convey them from the Château to the camp.

She had no intention of asking anyone to carry them because that would be to reveal immediately, when her Stepfather and mother began to look for her, where she had gone.

It would be quite easy for the Comte, driving his fast horses, to catch up with the gypsies, who would move slowly.

Valda was determined that she would not return home until she had proved very conclusively that she was capable of looking after herself and therefore capable of making up her own mind when it came to marriage.

"To be discovered too soon would defeat my whole object in leaving," she said to herself.

The trunks, valises, and bags were kept in a special room on the second floor, but Valda knew it would be impossible for her to take with her a trunk or even a valise, as they were all made of leather.

She then remembered that the house-maids had large brown-linen bags in which they put the various items of linen before they were sent downstairs to the laundry-maid to be washed.

One bag contained handkerchiefs, another ladies' underwear, a third was kept exclusively for gentlemen's garments.

The brown bags which were the size of small sacks were just what she needed, Valda thought.

She took one from the house-maids' cupboard, hid it on a top shelf where it would not be noticed, and decided it would be quite easy after everyone had gone to bed to pack it with the things she required.

There remained one other important item and that was money.

She only had a few hundred francs of her own and she was well aware that it would be very stupid to set off on such an expedition without being able to pay her way.

If things became too difficult she could either hire a carriage and drive home or take the train to Arles.

Either way, she could not expect to be conveyed on credit, and there was also the two hundred francs she had promised the gypsies and the fifty francs she was to pay for her board and lodging every day she was with them.

When she reached Saintes Maries de la Mer she might wish to stay at an Hotel. Anyway, there would be various expenses—that was inevitable—and she reckoned she would need at least fifteen hundred francs to feel safe and under no pressure to return home until she was ready to do so.

This was a problem that required a great deal of thought.

To ask for money when she obviously had nothing in particular to spent it on would be to arouse suspicion.

As it happened, Valda seldom paid cash for anything.

In Paris her mother or Stepfather had accounts at all the most important shops and if she went anywhere there was always someone to accompany her and pay the expenses.

She walked through the Château looking at the

wealth of treasures in every room and thought with a little smile to herself that it was not a question of "Water, water everywhere nor any drop to drink," but "Money, money everywhere nor any sou to spend"!

It was a problem that exercised her mind through most of the day.

She had luncheon with her mother and while Valda chatted away as she usually did of things which interested them both, one small part of her mind was busy with one question only—where could she obtain money?

She was quite certain of one thing, that her mother, even if she asked her, would have very little money with her.

The Comte took care of all the expenses of the Château, and although the Comtesse's fortune which she had inherited on her husband's death was undoubtedly used in one way or another, her husband had power of Attorney, and she did not even have to sign the cheques.

It was when she was growing almost desperate that Valda remembered the Estate Office that was situated at one end of the Château and presided over by *Monsieur* Févre, who managed the Estate for the Comte and was in fact both agent and manager.

When her mother had gone to rest before dinner Valda walked quickly through the long passages on the ground floor to reach the Estate Office.

It was a square room with walls covered in maps, furnished with a very large desk at which sat a middle-aged man who lived some two miles away in an attractive farm-house which had been converted for him and his family.

He looked up in surprise as Valda appeared.

"This is a pleasant surprise, *M'mselle* Valda!" he exclaimed. "And you have only just caught me. I was locking up."

"I thought you might be," Valda replied, "but I wanted to see you and Mama and I have been so busy all the afternoon."

"But of course I am at your disposal," *Monsieur* Févre said. "Will you not sit down?"

He indicated a seat on the other side of the desk.

"I feel rather like a prospective tenant," Valda said with a smile, "or perhaps one to whom you are giving a ticking off because his roof needs repair or his crops have failed."

"I hope I do not appear to be an ogre." *Monsieur* Févre smiled. "Most of our tenants are, I believe, quite contented people."

"And they pay their rents?"

"They do indeed!"

He glanced instinctively as he spoke at the safe which stood on the floor behind his desk.

"Are you not afraid if you keep the money here that someone will steal it?" Valda asked.

"I think that unlikely," *Monsieur* Févre replied. "As you know, there are three night-watchmen in the Château. The one on this floor visits the office several times during the night."

He looked at the windows.

"The shutters are closed when I leave, and bolted, and I also lock the door of the office."

"Do you take the keys home with you?" Valda asked.

"I used to," *Monsieur* Févre replied, "but the Agent of another Estate was robbed on his way home and the thieves entered the office of *Monsieur* de Touriet and stole everything they could find."

Valda laughed.

"They must have planned it very carefully and known when he was leaving."

"Exactly!" *Monsieur* Févre agreed. "And that is why your Stepfather and I decided the keys should be kept here."

"I think you are very wise," Valda said. "Where do you keep them?"

"When *Monsieur le Comte* is in residence I take him both the key of the safe and the key of the office," *Monsieur* Févre replied. "When you are all in Paris they are left with the Major-Domo. As you know, he has been in the service of the de Merlimonts since he was a boy, like his father and his grandfather before him."

"I see you have thought of everything, *Monsieur* Févre," Valda exclaimed. "But I think it is rather frightening to think there are thieves and robbers only waiting for a chance to carry away our precious possessions!"

She gave a little sigh as she added:

"I was only considering today how many treasures we have in this house."

"That is true, *M'mselle* Valda," *Monsieur* Févre agreed.

"Not only from a commercial point of view, but from the point of history," Valda said quickly. "They are all so much a part of the family that to lose them would be an inexpressible tragedy."

"It would indeed!" *Monsieur* Févre exclaimed.

Valda rose to her feet.

"There are so many things that I wanted to talk about with you, but I realise it is getting late and you want to return home. I really came to discuss the horses but they can wait until tomorrow."

"The horses?" *Monsieur* Févre exclaimed in surprise.

"Yes," Valda said. "I was thinking we should try and persuade *Beau-père* to buy more of the white horses from the Camargue. We have one, as you know, but Blanc-Blanc is getting old and they are so beautiful that I thought we could do with several more in the stable."

She knew as she spoke that the horses of the Camargue were one of *Monsieur* Févre's great enthusiasms, and she had almost forgotten it until she had wished for an excuse to talk to him.

Now his eyes lit up and he said:

"I have often regretted the fact that *Monsieur le Comte* was not as interested in the white horses of the Camargue as I would wish him to be. They are unique, and while he has listened to me about having black

Camargue cattle, he has never really enjoyed riding Blanc-Blanc."

"I think we must persuade him between us," Valda said. "Perhaps I could give him a Camargue mare as a present for his birthday or for Christmas."

"That is certainly an idea, *M'mselle* Valda!" *Monsieur* Févre exclaimed.

"We will talk about it another day," Valda said. "If you hear of one for sale, perhaps you would tell me about it and not mention it to *Beau-père*. It must be a surprise!"

"I am so delighted that they interest you, *M'mselle* Valda," *Monsieur* Févre said.

"It was just an idea I had when I was riding today," Valda told him, "but you will not say anything about it to *Beau-père,* will you? Not until we have my present ready for him."

"My lips are sealed!" *Monsieur* Févre said. "That I promise you."

Valda glanced at the clock on the mantelpiece.

"Again I must apologise for keeping you talking," she said, "and to save you time, give me the keys and I will take them to *Beau-père* myself. That will save you the walk back through the house."

"That is very kind of you, *M'mselle*," *Monsieur* Févre said, "but it is really no trouble."

"I am quite certain that your wife is watching the clock at home and wondering what is keeping you." Valda smiled. "It makes me feel guilty."

"It has been a pleasure to talk to you, *M'mselle* Valda."

Monsieur Févre opened the door of the office and Valda waited in the passage while he locked it. Then she held out her hand.

"Thank you very much, *M'mselle* Valda. It is very kind of you," *Monsieur* Févre said.

"It is my fault you have been detained," Valda answered, "so hurry home as fast as you can."

"I will do that." He smiled.

They moved away from each other in opposite directions.

Valda started to walk along the passage which led to the main part of the Château.

She had not gone far when she heard an outer door slam and knew that *Monsieur* Févre had left.

She waited for a few moments in case he should return, then hurrying back to the office she unlocked the door and entered, closing it behind her.

It only took her a few minutes to unlock the safe.

As she had expected, there was quite a large amount of banknotes of different denominations stacked in neat piles and there were small bags of coins on another shelf.

She took exactly fifteen hundred francs in notes and coins, and wrote an IOU on a small piece of paper which she put under a pile of notes, where she felt it would not be noticed until *Monsieur* Févre added up exactly what he had in the safe.

She had an idea that this would not be until the end of the month, when it was likely that after the tenants had paid their rents the money would be taken to the Bank in Arles.

Closing the safe again, Valda locked it and the office door, and moving quickly back into the main Hall approached one of the footmen on duty.

"Where is *Monsieur le Comte?*" she asked.

"He has just gone upstairs, *M'mselle,* to change for dinner."

This was what Valda had hoped to hear, and now she went into the Library where her Stepfather habitually sat and laid the keys in the centre of the blotter on his desk.

He would imagine, she thought, that *Monsieur* Févre had left them there before he went home and would not at any rate for the moment connect them with her.

Then conscious that she had been rather clever, she went upstairs to change for dinner.

Chapter Three

Seated in the front of the *Phuri Dai*'s caravan, Valda felt wildly excited as the procession of caravans moved slowly along the dusty road.

On either side the red earth of Provence showed beneath the olive groves, silver-green under the rising sun, and the grey, bare limestone rocks protruded like strange primordial tombstones above the red of the plains.

Poppies, lavender, wild thyme, and yellow gorse lined the road, and the almond trees were pink and white against the blue sky.

It was so beautiful that Valda felt she was walking into a fairy-tale which was all a part of her adventure.

Even now she could hardly believe that she had really started on the most momentous journey she had ever undertaken, and that she had really dared to leave her home to prove to her Stepfather that she was capable of looking after herself.

When she had crept downstairs before anyone in the Château was awake, dressed in her gypsy clothes, carrying her camera in one hand and her linen bag in the other, she felt desperately afraid that she would be unable to get away.

Someone was sure to see her and refuse to let her leave.

Any of the older servants would, she knew, if they saw her creeping out at such an early hour, wake her mother, feeling it their duty to inform the Comtesse that her daughter was behaving in a strange manner.

The house was very still.

The night-watchmen had made their rounds five minutes earlier. Valda had listened until they passed her door and she guessed they would then congregate in a small room downstairs where they drank tea or coffee to help keep themselves awake.

This was her opportunity and she hurried on tip-toe along the dark passage and down the back-stairs.

She did not attempt to leave through the kitchen-quarters just in case some scullery-maid had risen early to start the endless scrubbing of the flagged floors, which was one of the most arduous tasks in the Château.

Instead, she unbolted a door into the garden. It was seldom used so she hoped the fact that it had been unlocked might escape the notice of the household until later in the day.

Following her father's example, she had tried to think of every detail that would enable her to escape.

Outside her bed-room she had left a note saying:

"Please do not call me as I wish to sleep late."

That, she knew, would prevent anyone from entering her bed-room until at least ten or eleven o'clock in the morning.

On her dressing-table she had propped up a letter for her Stepfather.

She thought very carefully about what she would say before she wrote:

Dearest Beau-père,

I love you for your kindness and thought for me, but I cannot allow you to choose my husband. You told me yesterday that I was not capable of buying a gown without Mama's help or of journeying to Paris without being escorted by a Courier.

You also said that my qualifications did not include anything that was salable. This was a challenge, and I feel that if I can prove to you that I can do all these things on my own, without assistance from anyone, you will then agree that I am competent to choose the man with whom I must spend the rest of my life.

Please do not let Mama be too worried about me. I promise that if I am in any real difficulty I will come home at once.

My love, and do not be angry with your adventurous Stepdaughter,

Valda

She read the letter through very carefully to make quite certain she had made no mistakes.

She also felt that when her Stepfather read it he would be quite convinced she was on her way to Paris and would undoubtedly search for her there.

There was, however, a danger in that he would have expected her to take the train from Arles, and unless the gypsies had passed the city before he set out for the station, he might see their caravans and perhaps stop to enquire if they had seen her.

Then Valda told herself that such a course was very unlikely.

Although the Comte was quite prepared to offer the gypsies the hospitality of his land, which by tradition had been accorded them by every Comte de Merlimont for several centuries, he was not particularly interested in them as people.

He had in fact often laughed at Valda's interest in their history, and she was sure it would never cross his mind for one moment that she might travel with them, or ask their help in effecting her escape from home.

The gypsies themselves had been somewhat perturbed when they found "the friend" they were expecting was in fact Valda herself.

"Does *Monsieur le Comte* know that you are coming with us, *M'mselle?*" the *Vataf* asked.

"No," Valda answered frankly. "But I promise you, *Monsieur Vataf,* that if he discovers where I am he will not be angry with you, however annoyed he may be with me."

She knew that the *Vataf* was considering whether he should refuse to take her and quickly she presented

him with the five hundred francs she had promised.
Then before he could say any more she went in search
of the *Phuri Dai.*

The old gypsy also was surprised to see Valda.

"This is wrong, *M'mselle!*" she said. *"Monsieur le
Comte* and *Madame,* your mother, will be worried
about you."

"I want them to worry!" Valda answered. "I will tell
you why once we have started on our journey."

The *Phuri Dai* did not answer and after a moment
Valda said hastily:

"Please take me! I promise you there will be no unpleasant consequences and it is desperately important to
me."

She spoke with such sincerity that the *Phuri Dai*
stared at her until the uncertainty in her eyes changed
to a look of compassion.

"You know that we will help you if it is possible,"
the old gypsy said.

"Thank you," Valda answered. "All I ask is that I
may travel with you, if not as far as Saintes Maries de
la Mer, at least until I am far away from here."

She had thought during the night that perhaps it
would embarrass the gypsies if they should arrive at
Saintes Maries de la Mer with a *Gadjé.*

The twenty-fourth of May was essentially a gypsy
Festival and Valda had been thinking that perhaps she
would be wise to join them after the vigil in the crypt
was over and the Blessing of the Sea had been invoked.

However, all she was concerned with at the moment
was getting to the other side of Arles, and when the
Phuri Dai asked her into her own caravan she ac-
quiesced with pleasure, feeling she did not wish to answer questions or be concerned with the other gypsies.

A child took her first to the caravan that had been
allotted for her use.

It was a small one painted with gay signs in red,
white, and green, and drawn by a piebald horse with a
long mane and flowing tail.

The *Phuri-Dai*'s widowed daughter was already
seated in the front of it. She was a small, very dark-

skinned woman with shy eyes, and was, Valda guessed, not much older than she was herself.

Her husband had been killed in an accident and she had no children. Valda was to learn later that there were already several suitors in the tribe who were anxious to marry her.

At this moment she merely smiled at Valda and helped her to lift her camera and her linen bag into the caravan. Then Valda went back to join the *Phuri Dai* and the cavalcade started off.

The horses, having rested for forty-eight hours, were fresh and they moved comparatively swiftly along the narrow lane which led after about two miles onto the highway to Arles.

Valda sat just inside the caravan.

Although it was early in the morning there seemed to be a great number of people about, and she remembered that the women of Arles were noted as being the best-looking in all France.

"There is a strong strain of Roman blood in Arles mixed with the Greek and the Gallic," the Comte had said. "The Arles women know they are beautiful and do not allow anyone to forget it!"

He had laughed as he added:

"Even the fish-wives in the market-place feel they are Queens and bear themselves with their black mantillas cast over their arms in a queenly manner."

It was true, Valda noticed, that their straight brows and small noses looked Greek and they had magnificent dark eyes and thick black hair which framed their olive complexions.

"Have you ever seen the bull-baiting in the Amphitheatre?" the *Phuri Dai* asked.

Valda shook her head.

She had asked her Stepfather on several occasions if she could go but he had always refused.

The Amphitheatre was one of the sights of Arles and she had seen it often when it was empty.

It was said when it was built by the Romans to be able to hold thirty thousand spectators, which was more than the whole population of Arles at the moment.

There had been the three stages of seats, those for the Senators, those for the Knights, and the upper range for the ordinary people. These had now been turned into a promenade.

The people of Arles were passionately fond of bull-baiting and performances took place weekly throughout the Summer.

They were, Valda knew, quite different from the Spanish bull-fights. There was no brutality, no torture of the bulls with lances and crackers, and no goring of the horses.

"The bull is not injured, although he gets angry and wants to fight," the Comte had explained. "He enjoys the fight and in some cases cannot be induced to stop."

"Nevertheless, it is pointless!" Valda's mother had said.

"A lot of sport is that," the Comte remarked, "and although bull-baiting is not cruel I have no wish for either of you to see it."

On Saturdays Arles was very crowded and in the market there would gather the guardians—or managers of the herds; the *manadiers*—or owner-farmers; gypsies trying to sell horses; and Spaniards, Algerians, and Corsicans seeking employment on the farms.

And of course there would be Matadors with their unmistakable walk like a ballet-dancer!

The bulls which were baited came from the Camargue, the black bulls which Valda knew she would see there as well as the white horses.

She was not really worried that she might be discovered before they reached Arles, nevertheless she sighed with relief when finally they left the city behind and found themselves out in the Rhône Delta with the silver river on one side of them.

Cut off from the rest of France by the two main arms of the Rhone, which divides at Arles, the Camargue occupied an area of 140,000 acres.

Since a Roman gentleman Aulus Annivs Camars owned a big Estate there and called it *Insula Camarica,* it had hardly changed.

She was entering a district full of magic, legend, and romance—a mysterious wilderness on the coast of the Mediterranean, the realm of wild white horses and wild black bulls, of gypsies and pink flamingos.

"You have been here before, *M'mselle?*" the *Phuri Dai* asked.

"No, never," Valda answered, "but I have been looking forward to seeing it."

They were passing the rich farm-lands of vines, corn-fields, orchards, and pasture.

Every mile they journeyed brought them nearer to where Valda knew was a mosaic of lakes, reed-beds, pools, and salt steppes, and even now there seemed to be more birds and more flowers than there had been before.

But there were still quite a number of trees such as poplar, elm, willow, elder, and ash, and she knew that soon they would reach dry grass-lands, and the fresh-water marshes.

"It is very beautiful!" she said aloud.

"It is wild, like us!" the *Phuri Dai* said. "That is why we love coming here. We feel at home."

"And yet if you wished you could stay here all the year round," Valda remarked.

The *Phuri Dai* smiled.

"Always we must wander," she answered. "It is part of our life—moreover, we must earn our living."

"That is true," Valda agreed, "and yet it must some-times be sad to be always moving, always going some-where else."

"That is how we live," the *Phuri Dai* said simply. "Perhaps it is the curse of the gypsies, perhaps it is a blessing. It makes us find happiness amongst our-selves."

Valda thought later that evening, when they had camped for the night, how true that was.

They had found a field where a sign had told them they were welcome, not far from a large farm which was called a *Mas*.

It had the red-tiled roof of Provence and there were

cypress trees growing round it as a protection from the stormy winds which would sweep in from the sea in the Winter.

Most *Mas* in the Camargue, Valda was to learn, were protected with closely planted cypress trees or by thick leafy plane trees, which were also good for holding the dusty soil together.

And the flowers were very beautiful! There was wisteria growing over red walls as well as wild iris and orchids in the long high grasses which had not yet been cut for hay.

The farmer came out to speak to the gypsies and for the first time Valda saw a Camargue white horse being ridden with the big leather Camargue saddle.

Very high and wide in front and at the back, it was hand-made and embossed.

It had the long iron stirrup which she had been told was like those used by the mediaeval Crusaders.

The gypsies thanked the farmer for allowing them to camp, then he rode away and they started to unharness the horses and turn them free.

The women began to prepare the evening meal.

Soon Valda was aware of a delicious aroma coming from the black pots suspended on tripods over the fires.

There was not one fire but several, because even amongst the gypsies there was a protocol, so that the *Vataf,* the *Phuri Dai,* and their sons and daughters ate round one fire with Valda, while the gypsies of the other families encircled others.

Valda did not like to appear inquisitive by asking what they were about to eat, but when she tasted it she realised it was chicken and wondered which farm it had come from.

Indeed, it might have been the cockerel she had given the *Vataf* yesterday.

It was, however, cooked in a way she had never tasted before, and as if she realised what she was thinking the *Phuri Dai* explained:

"The gyspies use a great many herbs in cooking, and there are nettles in this dish, besides vegetables which grow wild, and of course mushrooms."

"What happens when you cannot get a chicken or even a rabbit?" Valda asked.

The *Vataf* smiled.

"Then we have to find a *niglo*," he answered.

Valda knew that in English this meant a hedgehog, and she remembered she had been told that it was a very popular dish amongst the gypsies and always eaten on festive occasions.

She was glad however that they were not eating one tonight.

She had the feeling that she did not wish to eat hedgehog, even though living in France she had so often watched people enjoying frogs' legs and snails.

There was no bread with the chicken stew, but a maize cake which was perfumed with seeds and curry.

"The *ankruste* is particularly enjoyed amongst the *Kalderash*," the *Phuri Dai* explained.

Valda found it quite palatable although she thought she would have preferred ordinary bread.

She was not offered wine with the meal as she had expected, seeing that the gypsies were French, but instead they drank cups of tea.

Several times during the journey one of the younger gypsies had come to the *Phuri Dai*'s caravan to bring her a cup of boiling-hot tea. Valda had noticed that the way the gypsies drank was to pour it out little by little into the saucer and lap it up noisily.

All the day they had been travelling the *Phuri Dai* had been smoking her pipe; but she had not used tobacco but instead a mixture of herbs and dried leaves ground up together.

It had a very pleasant smell, but when the *Phuri Dai* asked Valda if she would like to smoke she shook her head.

"You are right, *M'mselle*," the *Phuri Dai* said, "women should not smell of smoke. It is a bad habit, but one I enjoy!"

She laughed as she went on:

"We all have our bad habits, otherwise life would be very dull."

"I cannot believe you ever find it dull," Valda said.

"It is we who are shut up in houses as if in cages who have a dull existence."

Her face had been very expressive as she spoke, and after a moment the *Phuri Dai* asked:

"Why are you running away, *M'mselle?*"

"Because my Stepfather wishes me to be married in the French manner to a man I have never seen, simply because socially it would be advantageous to us both."

There was silence after she had spoken.

The *Phuri Dai* was sitting staring ahead at the road, her hands holding the reins loosely, the horses moving much as they wished to do.

"It is wrong!" Valda went on. "Wrong at any rate as far as I am concerned! I refuse to marry a man I do not love!"

"And suppose you never find one?" the *Phuri Dai* asked.

"Then perhaps it would be better not to marry at all!"

The old woman turned her face to look at Valda and smiled.

"There is no need for you to worry, *M'mselle*. You'll find a man who is your mate because that is nature's way. Look at the ducks, the storks, the partridges, the gulls, the egrets. At this time of year the males have found their females and are building their nests. What is natural for them is natural for us!"

"That is what I feel," Valda answered.

She thought of the owls that had hooted last night as she had been making up her mind what she must do.

"Life is never easy," the *Phuri Dai* went on. "We have to fight for what we want, perhaps suffer, but in the end it is worthwhile."

"You are saying exactly what I want to hear," Valda said. "To accept tamely what is suggested would, to my mind, be cowardly, besides being a certain path to unhappiness."

"What you are seeking is love," the *Phuri Dai* said. "That is what all women want, the love of a man who has sought you out because you are his woman and he is your man."

Valda drew in her breath.

"Yes. That is what I want. That is what I seek."

"Then you'll find it," the *Phuri Dai* said.

"Are you sure of that?"

"I'm sure!" the *Phuri Dai* replied.

Valda wondered whether she should ask the old woman to read her future in the cards and perhaps look at her palm; but even as she thought it the *Phuri Dai* showed that she knew her thoughts by saying:

"It is best not to know one's fate. If you are uncertain or afraid, it can give you confidence. But if you have faith in yourself, you know without sorcery that your life will be full, and you can attract to yourself what you are prepared to give."

Valda pondered on this for some time, then she said:

"You mean if I am prepared to give love I shall receive it?"

"That is the law of nature," the *Phuri Dai* answered. "Each gives, each receives. Only for those who do not give is there an empty heart, an empty soul."

"I understand," Valda said.

She felt a little warmth inside her because the *Phuri Dai* had put into words and confirmed what she felt herself.

'I am setting out on my own Crusade,' she thought, 'in search of love, in search of the fullness of life.'

She turned shining eyes towards the *Phuri Dai*.

"I am so glad I was brave enough to come."

"We all need courage," the gypsy answered. "Without it we would sink into insignificance and be lost."

Valda thought how brave the gypsies had been through centuries of persecution.

Despite all efforts to stamp them out, to imprison them, to drive them from country to country, they had survived and remained a formidable people with their own customs, their own crafts, and even their own religion.

What was more, they were, despite what people said about them, far more moral than most of those who abused them.

Valda had known when she had asked the gypsies if she could travel with them that she would have nothing to fear from the gypsy men.

For one thing, she was a *Gadjé* and therefore forbidden to them. For another, the gypsies married very young and there was no question of a man being unfaithful to his wife or his wife to him.

There were very strict penalties imposed by the elders or the leader of a tribe on any gypsy who behaved immorally or brought discredit to his tribe.

They might steal, and they certainly poached because a gypsy believed that God had given the wild creatures to those who needed them. But a gypsy seldom committed murder, and crimes against women were not to be found imputed to them in any police records.

"Your people have great courage!" Valda said aloud.

"We have needed it," the *Phuri Dai* said simply.

As she spoke Valda remembered that in the previous century the gypsies in the Basque country were obliged to wear a red helmet marked with a goat's-foot and sentenced to go bare-foot.

Even those who were Catholics had a segregated place reserved for them in the Churches where they had to take the Holy water with a stick.

When the meal round the fire was finished the gypsies began to sing a love-song, which after a few minutes was accompanied on a violin skilfully played by a young gypsy boy of about sixteen years of age.

"That is my grandson," the *Vataf* said proudly. "He is a musician and he plays with his heart."

"Has he had lessons?" Valda asked.

The *Vataf* shook his head.

"It is born in him," he said. "All gypsies love music and when we get to Saintes Maries de la Mer the girls will dance. They are very graceful."

The gypsy playing the violin was joined by another with a pipe. More women began to sing, and now it was not so much a song as a rhythmic chant and seemed somehow appropriate to the darkness round them and the stars overhead.

Valda wondered what it would feel like to be here at this moment with a man who loved her.

She could imagine nothing more romantic than to listen to the gypsy music and know that she was close to a man to whom she thrilled when she felt his touch.

She felt it so vividly that her dream seemed almost like reality.

Then the *Phuri Dai* rose from beside the fire, moving slowly and with difficulty because her leg hurt her.

"It is time for bed," she said, "and you, *M'mselle,* must have a good sleep because we shall be on the road early again tomorrow morning."

"Then I, too, had better go to bed," Valda said.

She said good-night both to the *Vataf* and to the *Phuri Dai* and climbed into her own caravan.

It had been set alongside the *Phuri Dai*'s and they were both a little apart from the rest of the tribe.

It was very simply furnished. There was a mattress on the floor and two blankets with which to cover herself and a pillow with a linen cover on it.

It was all very clean and smelt sweetly of herbs, a bunch of which was hanging from the ceiling.

There was a curtain heavy as a blanket to draw over the front of the caravan and pretty cotton curtains for the little window high on one side. There were a few shelves from which everything had been removed while they were travelling.

There was a wool mat on the floor and Valda found that a basin and a pitcher of water had been placed inside for her.

She knew this was a concession which would not have been made to the other gypsies, who, if they washed, would use a stream or perhaps a pump.

Valda took off her red skirt, her full petticoats, and her embroidered blouse. Then she hesitated before she removed her other garments.

She was quite certain that the gypsies would not do so, but she told herself there was no reason why she should behave any differently from how she would at home.

She put on her night-gown and slipped under the

blankets to find the mattress surprisingly comfortable.

Always at home she knelt beside her bed to say her prayers, but here she felt it would seem strange to kneel when her bed was flat on the floor, so she said her prayers lying down.

They were very different from the conventional ones she usually used. Now she asked that she should be safe, unafraid, and that she should not be discovered.

"Help me, God," she prayed, "to prove to *Beaupère* that I am both sensible and competent to do what I wish to do. And help me to find a man who will love me and not want me just because I have money."

That, she knew as she said it, was more important than anything else.

Even if a man said he loved her, how could she ever believe that he would have felt the same if she had been penniless and was not offered to him with her glittering fortune as an embellishment?

'If Papa had had a son,' she thought, 'things would have been very different. Most of his money would have gone to my brother, and I would have had just enough to be comfortable.'

She thought it over and decided that when she married she would have a large family: lots of sons, but only a few daughters!

Then, although she was half-asleep, she laughed.

"I have first to find them a father!"

She remembered the *Phuri Dai*'s words.

"It is nature's way that everyone should find their mate!"

* * *

The morning was sunless and rather chill as they set off soon after dawn. The boiling-hot tea which Valda drank as the gypsies drank theirs, because they were all in a hurry, from the saucer, made her feel warm and comfortable.

She ate *ankruste* spread with butter as the *Phuri Dai* drove her caravan after the *Vataf*, who led the way.

As soon as they had left the *Mas* with its cultivated

fields they began to see shallow waters and grass-lands which were a riot of daisies, clover, scarlet pimpernels, blue flags, and wild gladioli.

Where these stretches of grass-land had not been grazed too heavily by the cattle there was mock privet, with its dark, narrow, ever-green leaves gaining a foot-hold.

Now Valda could see the first of the purple herons and the oyster-catchers, besides the black-winged stilts, the elegant white egrets, golden plovers, and various wading-birds.

"They are on their Spring migration," the *Phuri Dai* explained, following the direction of her eyes.

"What I want to see are the pink flamingos," Valda said.

"You will see them further on," the *Phuri Dai* answered.

Valda kept looking over the shallow waters for what she knew would seem like a pink barrier, for in all France it is only in the Camargue that the pink flamingos breed.

They journeyed on, not stopping to eat at midday although the gypsies brought the *Phuri Dai* and Valda the inevitable hot tea and maize cakes eaten with a kind of pâte made from some unidentifiable animal.

It was delicious, but Valda was afraid to ask what it was in case she was told it was hedgehog.

Nevertheless, she ate it hungrily and enjoyed the tea, the gypsies coming up the road several times to refill their cups.

Now they saw ahead of them the village of Albaron, and when they had reached it there suddenly was the real Camargue.

There were its *étangs,* or lagoon-like expanses of water, its rugged salt-rock and long savanna.

"I think," Valda exclaimed suddenly, "that I should leave you here. I am sure this is where I shall find the wild horses that I wish to photograph. Then after you have had your Festival at Saintes Maries de la Mer, I will, if I may, join up with you again."

She thought, although she was not certain, that the *Phuri Dai* was relieved at her decision.

"It is over twenty miles, *M'mselle,* to Saintes Maries de la Mer," she said. "But if you wish to join us again I am sure there will be a carrier of some sort between Albaron and Saintes Maries."

"I am sure there will," Valda agreed. "So may I thank you, *Madame,* for your kindness, and will you accept the money I owe for being with you for two days?"

She had drawn out the forty francs as she spoke, but the *Phuri Dai* waved them away.

"There is no need for money to pass between friends," she said. "You and your family befriend my people and ask nothing in return. When you travel with us you travel as one of us."

"Thank you," Valda said. "You are very kind and I am very grateful for your help."

"Take care of yourself, *M'mselle,*" the *Phuri Dai* said. "I will pray for you to the Blessed Sara! I will pray that you will find what you seek, and that you will be happy."

"Thank you," Valda said again.

The *Phuri Dai* drew her horses to a standstill and Valda stepped down.

She walked back to the caravan behind and took from the *Phuri Dai*'s daughter her camera and bag.

Again she expressed her thanks. As the cavalcade moved on she stood watching them until the dust made her cough. Then she turned and walked along the road leading Eastward.

She knew from a map it ran along the top of the Étang de Vaccarès, the largest inland lagoon of the Camargue.

Although she had enjoyed herself with the gypsies there was something exciting in feeling that now she was completely on her own.

She saw a herd of black Camargue cattle in the distance, but she was not particularly interested in them.

There were a dozen varieties of wild duck on the

étangs and Valda recognised the sheldrake, widgeon, pochard, tufted, and pintail.

There were also cranes and teal, and a weasel ran across the road in front of her.

She walked on until suddenly on her left she was attracted by a flash of white.

She stood still, drawing in her breath, then realised she had not been mistaken.

A number of white Camargue horses were grazing lazily on the sodden grasses which were like islands surrounded by water only a few inches deep.

Valda considered what she should do.

The horses were some way away. Then as she watched they appeared to be moving towards her. In fact she saw two other horses join them and she had the idea that they might move towards the still, flat water of Étang de Vaccarès, which was on the other side of the road.

On the other hand, they might gallop away and she might never have the chance of photographing such a large number again.

There were some stumpy mock-privet bushes on small islands of grass and there were also patches of bullrushes and tamarisk.

The tamarisk thrived, as Valda knew, only on the edges of lakes or ditches carrying fresh water, and as it was May they were covered with pink blossoms.

She thought that these might conceal the brilliance of her red skirt and the white of her blouse.

Putting down the linen bag next to a bush at the side of the road, she took off her red leather shoes and pulled down her stockings which she had worn out of modesty although they were out of keeping with her gypsy dress.

She put them beside the bag and picked up her camera.

She would have to wade towards the horses, in order to keep out of sight of them, behind the clumps of plants and shrubs if she was to get near enough for a photograph.

She looked round and seeing no-one in sight pulled her skirt with its voluminous petticoats up to her knees and stepped into the water.

It was not cold as she had expected, but warm from the hot sun, and she guessed that it was a mixture of both sea and fresh water.

The Kodak camera was not heavy to carry.

Since the exposure was much quicker in this new model, Valda was sure that unless the horses were galloping at a tremendous speed she would be able to get a good picture of them.

Certainly she was going to try! And once again she thought, if she could only have an Exhibition in Paris of the snapshots she had taken in the Camargue, what a very persuasive answer it would be to her Stepfather's allegation that she had no qualifications which were salable.

After she had waded through the water a little way she found herself on the grass, but unfortunately there were no more bushes to conceal her.

The grass itself was however so high that by lying down in it and crawling along she was, she thought, completely hidden.

She did not dare move quickly in case she made a noise, but she covered quite a lot of ground until finally she found that she was near enough to the horses to be almost sure they were within photographing range.

At the same time, she was aware that a stallion had raised his head, and she knew that he must have sensed danger. Unless she was to drive them away she must keep very still.

Valda held her breath, peering through the grasses where she could see the horses clearly, and realised their beauty had not been exaggerated.

They were not very large. In fact most of them seemed smaller even than the horse her Stepfather owned, and she guessed that the majority were only about fourteen hands high.

They were, however, thick-set, and she could understand how they were known as the strongest horses ever bred.

Their necks were muscular, their brows wide, and their eyes very deep-set. But the long manes and the tails which swept the ground were the things which gave the horses their character and their nobility.

'No wonder they look as if they should be ridden by the gods!' Valda thought to herself.

She lay watching them, thinking there had never been more beautiful animals, until almost with a start she realised she had been so occupied admiring the horses that she had not yet photographed them.

Slowly, moving hardly more than an inch at a time, she crept a little nearer until she found that she was in fact on the very edge of the grassy island.

Between her and the horses there was an expanse of water but by pushing her camera in front of her she could focus it on them.

There was a view-finder and very slowly, so that she would not attract attention by her movements, Valda raised her head to look through it.

When she could see clearly enough that she could take a perfect picture of the horses grouped together, another stallion had his head still up and Valda dropped her own.

Then as her hand crept forward to press the shutter-release there was the sound of galloping hoofs behind her and as she turned her head apprehensively the horses in front of her moved away.

She gave a little cry of fear for now she saw that the hoofs she had heard were almost upon her. In fact it seemed to her that at any moment she would be trampled.

Instinctively, hardly aware of what she was doing, she raised herself to her knees.

She had a quick impression of a horse coming straight at her. Then as she screamed in sheer terror she fell backwards off the grassy island and into the shallow water beyond it.

The water splashed round her and she screamed

again. Then she saw that the horse that had galloped up behind her was being ridden by a man.

To Valda, half-lying in the water, her face splashed and her camera beside her, he seemed dark and sinister.

His horse was white, and he was riding it with the usual long iron stirrups, his legs stretched almost to full length.

Because she was frightened and disconcerted by what had happened, Valda said the first words that came into her head.

"Why could you not have looked where you were going?" she asked furiously. "You might have killed me!"

She spoke in French and he replied:

"What in the name of God do you mean by hiding yourself in the grass? I had no idea anyone was there."

Valda sat up in the water and reached for her camera, which was floating serenely on the surface.

"You have ruined the picture I was taking!"

The man had drawn his horse to a standstill. Now he said in a different tone:

"You are a photographer?"

"I was trying to be!" Valda said crossly. "Only you have spoilt it!"

She raised herself to her feet as she spoke, realising that her skirt was soaked and so was the back of her blouse. Even the red handkerchief which had covered her hair now hung dripping down her back.

She pulled it off and looked at it ruefully. Then the man sitting on the horse watching her said after a moment:

"You do not look like a gypsy even if you are dressed like one! And I have never heard of a gypsy taking photographs!"

"I am not a gypsy!" Valda snapped. "As it happens, *je suis Anglaise!*"

"That explains it!" the man said in English. "I have never seen a gypsy or a French woman with red hair and blue eyes."

For the first time Valda looked at him directly and

realised that, while he had seemed dark because he had menaced her on his horse, he was in fact very un-French in appearance.

"You are English?" she queried.

"Like you," he replied.

"Then perhaps you can tell me if there is an Inn nearby where I could get my clothes dried."

As Valda spoke she had the idea that his eyes were twinkling. She realised she must in fact look very strange, practically soaked to the skin and bare-legged beneath her red gypsy skirt.

"As I am responsible for your plight," the man on the horse said, "the least I can do is to offer you my horse to convey you to the *Mas* where I am staying myself. It is not far. Not more than two miles away."

Valda was about to reply that she had no wish to trouble him, when she told herself that it would serve him right if she did put him to a lot of trouble.

She did not mind being wet half so much as losing the picture, and she thought despairingly that she might never have an opportunity again of finding so many of the Camargue horses together.

"My shoes are on the roadside," she said coldly. "I will walk as far as that. Then I should be glad to avail myself of your offer."

"Very sensible," the man approved. "After all, you do not wish to catch cold, but I am afraid your pretty fancy-dress is spoilt."

There was something about the way in which he said "fancy-dress" which annoyed Valda.

After all, it was none of his business if she wished to walk about the Camargue dressed like a gypsy, and she was hoping that besides losing the picture, the whole film had not been spoilt when the camera had fallen into the water.

She had two more rolls of film in her bag, but she fancied from what she had seen of the Camargue that she would need every one of the three hundred exposures she could take with three films.

Besides which, she had hoped later to get some pictures of the gypsies at Saintes Maries de la Mer.

She walked ahead of the man on the horse without speaking. When she reached the road she found her linen bag and her shoes beside the bush.

She picked up her stockings and garters and slipped them into the bag, then put on her shoes and did up the straps.

As she straightened herself she realised the man had dismounted from his horse and was standing in the roadway, holding it.

She walked towards him.

He took the camera and the bag from her and she waited almost imperiously for him to help her into the saddle.

She expected him to cup his hands in the correct manner, but instead he laid down the bag and the camera and putting his hands on each side of her small waist, swung her up without any effort.

Not into the saddle but onto the horse's bare back behind it.

Then he fastened her bag to the pummel and looked up at her. She saw that his eyes were twinkling with amusement.

"Are you still angry with me?" he enquired.

"Yes, I am!"

"I am very contrite!"

"So you should be! I may never again have a chance of getting such a picture of the wild horses."

"You will!"

"How can you be sure?"

"I will take you to a far better place to photograph them."

Valda's anger evaporated.

"Will you really do that?" she asked, and her voice was eager and excited.

"Only if you stop being cross with me," the man replied. "I have a strong aversion to disagreeable women!"

Valda laughed. She could not help it.

"I will not be cross," she promised.

Chapter Four

He swung himself up in front of her onto the heavy saddle, holding the camera in his hand.

As he picked up the reins of the white horse, who had stood quite still since Valda had been put on his back, he asked:

"You are not nervous? You have ridden before?"

"I have ridden since I was five," Valda answered almost indignantly.

"I apologise," he said with a note of laughter in his voice.

The horse moved off and Valda realised that they were deliberately going slowly in case she should slip off the back of the horse and onto the ground.

It annoyed her when she was such an exceptional horse-woman, and yet she had to admit, it was considerate of him.

"So he ought to be!" she told herself, feeling her blouse clinging damply to her back and realising that her skirt was soaked right through to her skin.

As she looked at the back of the man in front of her she thought he must be a guardian.

Monsieur Févre when talking of the Camarque horses and their guardians, had told her that their Patron Saint was St. George.

"It is most appropriate," he had said, "a guardian riding a white horse, armed with a long lance which could easily be a trident, when warding off a wild Camargue bull could easily be attacking a dragon!"

Valda thought that the Englishman was really too tall for his Camargue horse, and yet even when riding

with the long stirrup she guessed that he was a good
rider and would, mounted on an English horse, perhaps
be exceptional.

He wore an old worn tweed jacket and long mud-
splashed boots, but she could imagine that when he was
dressed for one of the Festivals of the Guardians in
hound's-tooth moleskin breeches, black velvet jacket, a
traditional blue shirt with a flower motif, and short
Spanish-style boots he would be very impressive.

As if he somehow sensed she was thinking about him
the Englishman said over his shoulder:

"Perhaps we should introduce ourselves. My name is
Roydon Sanford."

"Mine is Valda Bu . . ."

Valda hesitated.

Because he was English, she felt it might be unwise
to tell him her real name.

It was unlikely he would have heard of her father. At
the same time, Sir Edward had been a well-known personality and the newspapers had constantly reported
his exploits.

". . . Burton!" she finished.

"And you are a photographer," Roydon Sanford
said. "Do you work for any particular magazine?"

Valda realised he thought she was a reporter and
smiled to herself.

"I am taking snapshots for an Exhibition," she replied, thinking as she spoke that that at least partly
was true.

"In London?" he questioned.

"Perhaps," she replied. "But actually I thought Paris
would be more interested in pictures of the Camargue.
I only hope you have not spoilt my film."

"I hope so too."

"I had an excellent view of the horses," she said
reproachfully.

"I have promised to compensate you for what I am
certain would have been a masterpiece," Roydon Sanford said, "by ensuring you will get a far better view not
only of the horses but also of the flamingos."

"I shall make you keep your promise! I hope you are not boasting."

"I am a most efficient guide," Roydon Sanford answered. "Where are you staying?"

"I . . . I had hoped to find a convenient Inn not far from here," Valda replied.

"There are not many Inns in the Camargue where a woman could stay alone," Roydon Sanford said after a moment, "but I dare say I could persuade *Madame* Porquier to accommodate you."

"Does she keep an Inn?" Valda enquired.

"No, indeed, she would be insulted by the idea! Her husband breeds cattle and has a *Mas* where I stay."

"It sounds interesting. Do you like working for them?"

"I am here on holiday," Roydon Sanford replied. "Because this is my third visit, they allow me to work with the guardians and ride their horses."

Valda was about to ask what he did at other times; then she thought it sounded somehow too inquisitive when she was speaking to a man's back and not his face.

She was silent and after a moment Roydon Sanford asked:

"Are you feeling cold? If you hold on tightly either to the back of the saddle or to me we will go a little faster."

"I have already told you there is no likelihood of my falling off," Valda answered. "I am not cold, but still unpleasantly wet!"

"Then we must certainly get you to the *Mas* quickly so that you can change."

He spurred the horse into a trot, and it was difficult to have any further conversation until they had moved off the road and across a field where in front of them was a *Mas,* or homestead, which in the Camargue was technically known as a *maison à terre*.

It was protected by the usual barrier of cypresses and shaded by plane trees and the flowers were even more beautiful than those Valda had noticed round the farm where they had camped the night before.

Here there was a profusion of blue flags and crimson gladioli, besides purple wisteria, golden honeysuckle, and climbing roses growing over the walls and even up the trunks of the trees.

Roydon Sanford rode past the house and turned into the yard at the back. Then he dismounted lithely and turned to lift Valda down.

As she stood beside him she realised that she had not noticed before that he was in fact tall, so tall that she had to tip back her head to look up at him.

He was however concerned with taking her linen bag from the saddle. Carrying it and the camera, he led the way across the yard to a door which opened into a big kitchen.

There was a beamed ceiling with hams and bunches of onions hanging from it, a stove occupying a large part of one wall, and a table in the centre of the flagged floor on which a plump woman was rolling out pastry with a wooden rolling-pin.

She looked up in surprise as Roydon Sanford entered and remarked:

"You are back early, *Monsieur!*"

"I have returned with someone who needs your assistance, *Madame,*" he answered. "Owing to a slight accident, she fell into the water and is very wet!"

The woman looked at Valda and the smile faded from her face.

"A *Caraque!*" she ejaculated.

"No, *Madame,*" Roydon Sanford said firmly, "an English woman. She is merely dressed as a gypsy for some reason I have not yet been able to discern."

"An English woman, *Monsieur!*" the woman exclaimed. "And a friend?"

"That is what I hope she will be," Roydon Sanford answered with twinkling eyes, "when she has forgiven me for spoiling the photograph she was taking with her camera."

He held it up as he spoke.

"You see, *Madame,* she has what is known as a snapshot camera, and she wishes to photograph the white horses."

"She is not the first," *Madame* replied, apparently unimpressed.

She wiped her hands on her apron, and Roydon Sanford, walking to the table, said:

"Let me introduce *Madame* Porquier, Miss Valda Burton."

Valda held out her hand.

"As *Monsieur* Sanford has told you," she said, "he frightened me on his horse and caused me to fall into the water. I should be grateful if you would allow me to change my clothes and dry my wet ones."

"But of course, *M'mselle*," *Madame* Porquier answered. "If you will come this way."

Roydon Sanford handed to Valda her linen bag.

"I will wipe the camera dry for you," he said, "but I do not think that the water will have percolated through its leather case."

"I hope you are right," Valda said coldly.

She knew she would be extremely annoyed if one of her films was damaged so that she could not use it.

They had of course been speaking in French, and now he added in English:

"I will leave you to make arrangements with *Madame* Porquier to stay here. I am sure, now that she realises you are not a gypsy, you will be very welcome."

Valda was about to reply that there was no need for him to wait and he could return to what he was doing before he had upset her. Then she thought that there might be a chance of taking some photographs before the afternoon was over.

"Please wait," she said. "I shall not be long."

The house formed a rectangular block, as was usual in farm-houses.

Valda had visited quite a number on her Stepfather's Estate and she knew that most of them were divided into two parts by a corridor down the middle.

On the ground floor, beside the large communal kitchen and a variety of larders there was the one comfortable room which served as a Reception- and Dining-Room, where members of the family congregated only when they were wearing their best clothes.

Sometimes there were two staircases and the rooms upstairs were arranged so that they were protected from the winds, which could at times be not only cold but overpowering.

The walls, which looked towards the sea, would, Valda was sure, be windowless except when the trees were high and strong enough to be a good wind-break.

Going up an old staircase of polished wood, *Madame* Porquier came to a landing on which, as far as Valda could see, there were only two doors.

She opened the one on the left and Valda found a delightful room containing the traditional large square curtained bed that the French always made comfortable with a number of goose-feather mattresses.

There were curtains over the window and outside strong wooden shutters that could be fastened at night, and for the Winter months there was a fireplace big enough to burn logs.

The floor was covered with a mixture of mats, some of white sheep-skin and others of coloured wools that the housewives in all parts of France make in the long Winter evenings.

It was spotlessly clean, everything shining with soap and beeswax, and through the open windows there was the fragrance of honeysuckle and roses mixed with the tang of salt from the Mediterranean.

"You can change here, *M'mselle,*" *Madame* Porquier said, looking curiously at the brown linen bag Valda carried.

"Thank you very much," Valda said. "And would it be possible for you to dry the clothes I am wearing?"

"But of course, *M'mselle!*"

"*Monsieur* Sanford did say that you might be kind enough to put me up for the night," Valda ventured.

Madame Porquier looked surprised.

"You are travelling alone, *M'mselle?*"

"I have friends whom I am meeting later at Saintes Maries de la Mer," Valda said. "I thought it would be wise to arrive after the Festival, as I am not a gypsy."

Madame laughed.

"It was your clothes that deceived me, *M'mselle.*

Now that I see your hair and your eyes, you do not
look in the least like a *Caraque!*"

"Then I may stay?" Valda enquired.

"It will be a pleasure, *M'mselle!* Any friend of *Monsieur* Sanford is always welcome!"

She spoke with a note of respect in her voice that
Valda did not miss.

"There is water in the jug, *M'mselle*," *Madame* Porquier went on, "and if you will be kind enough to bring
your wet clothes down to the kitchen I will hang them
in the sunshine. Or, if it is necessary, I will dry them
over the stove."

"I am sure they will dry very quickly in the sun."
Valda smiled.

"Please ask for anything you want, *M'mselle*," *Madame* Porquier said.

She went from the bed-room, closing the door behind
her, and Valda heard her footsteps going down the un-
covered wooden stairs.

She slipped off her skirts, glad to be rid of the cold
wetness of them.

She had to take off everything she was wearing, and
she noticed that the red from her skirt had run a little
into the first of the petticoats she wore underneath.

Her white blouse was stained from the grasses or
perhaps from the water itself in the *étang* into which
she had fallen.

When she was partially redressed in fresh under-
clothes she carried her blouse to the basin and tried to
wash it in cold water.

It was the first time in her life she had ever washed
anything for herself.

She thought she was doing it somewhat inadequately
and perhaps it would be better to ask *Madame* Porquier to do it for her.

"I can pay for anything I want," she told herself
reassuringly.

Her gypsy skirt had two deep pockets on either side,
into which she had put her money.

There had also been some in her linen bag, and now
as she looked at it lying on the dressing-table she won-

dered how she could stow it away in the thin Summer dress that she had brought with her.

When she packed she had chosen her gowns with great care.

There would be no lady's-maid to press them if they were creased, and as they had to be very light it was essential for her to make the right choice.

She had stood for a long time in front of her wardrobe packed with gowns of all sorts and descriptions.

Finally she had chosen two simple muslins which she thought would not look too expensive, though in fact they had come from a famous Parisian Couturier.

Two day-gowns and one for the evening was all Valda had allowed herself. But she had put in one of her thin riding-skirts with its light jacket which she wore in the heat of the Summer.

She debated now as to whether she should put this on. Then she thought that Mr. Sanford would not be expecting her to ride and later she could discuss the possibility of her doing so tomorrow.

She therefore went downstairs carrying her wet gypsy clothes and wearing a muslin gown which had a pattern of small blue flowers and a blue waist-band.

She had rearranged her hair, which had been crushed and flattened by the gypsy handkerchief.

As she walked into the kitchen where Roydon Sanford was sitting talking to *Madame* Porquier, he had an irrepressible look of admiration in his eyes as he rose to his feet.

"I have brought down my wet clothes as you suggested, *Madame*," Valda said to *Madame* Porquier. "I tried to wash the stains from my blouse, but I am afraid I have not done it very efficiently."

"I will do it for you, *M'mselle*," *Madame* Porquier replied, taking the clothes from Valda.

"Thank you," Valda said, and turned to Roydon Sanford to ask, "You have looked at the camera? It is all right?"

"As far as I can see, not a spot of water has gone through the leather cover," he replied. "It might be a wise precaution to change the film, but I am almost prepared to swear that it is quite undamaged."

"Then I will take your word for it," Valda said.

She had deliberately left upstairs the two other films she carried with her, because in the outer boxes which contained them she had hidden most of her money.

It was impossible, now that she had no pockets in her skirt, to walk about with so many franc notes.

Instead she had placed the films at the back of the drawer in her dressing-table and hidden them under the few things she was not wearing, like handkerchiefs and stockings.

She could not believe that anyone in this house was what her father had always called "light-fingered."

At the same time, she had to be careful.

To have all her money stolen at the outset of her adventure would force her to return home before she was ready to do so.

As an added precaution she put one note of five hundred francs in the bodice of her gown between her small breasts.

"No-one," she told herself with pride, "could accuse me of not being sensible and thinking of every detail."

"*Madame* has suggested," Roydon Sanford was saying, "that you might like a cup of coffee and one of her famous meat pasties. It is always wise to eat after an accident."

"I would like a cup of coffee," Valda answered, "but I am in fact not very hungry."

"You will be, after the first taste of one of *Madame*'s pasties!" Roydon Sanford answered.

He was speaking in French, which Valda knew was out of courtesy to his hostess.

"I will bring them to you in the Salon," *Madame* said.

"We are quite content to have them here," Roydon Sanford replied.

"You may eat with us when you are alone, *Monsieur*," *Madame* Porquier said in a tone of a reproving Nanny, "but when you have company you eat in the

Salon. Take *M'mselle* in there and I will bring your coffee within a minute or two."

Valda could not help thinking that *Madame*'s tone towards her had become far more respectful since she had changed and now looked more conventional and certainly more respectable than when she'd been wearing her gypsy clothes.

It was strange, she thought, how people despised the gypsies; and yet to her they had been everything that was kind, friendly, and helpful.

Roydon Sanford had opened another door of the kitchen for her and she walked through it into the Salon, which was a larger and more formal room.

There was something stiff and rather unlived-in about the furniture stuffed with horse-hair. And the aquatints of bulls and horses that could be bought in any provincial town bore very little resemblance to the beautiful wild animals they depicted.

"I gather you have persuaded *Madame* to let you stay?" Roydon Sanford said as he followed Valda across the room to the window where she stood looking out onto the flower-filled garden.

"She told me that any friend of yours was welcome," Valda said. "You are obviously persona grata. Why do you come here for your holidays?"

"I might just as well ask you why you have come to the Camargue," he answered. "The answer is because it is the most beautiful place either of us is likely to find anywhere in the world."

"I have not yet seen very much of it," Valda said, "but I feel what you have said is true."

"It has a magic which is indescribable. Once you have been here you long to return. Sometimes I find myself dreaming of the Camargue. Then I know that nothing will stop me from going back."

"This is my first visit," Valda said, "and so only when I have left will I be able to discover if it draws me as it draws you."

He did not reply and she knew without looking at him that his eyes were on her face.

"You are very young to travel alone," he said after a moment. "Why does your father permit it?"

"My father is dead!"

"But surely someone . . . ?" he began, then stopped. "It is not my business, but quite frankly you are too pretty not to need someone looking after you."

Valda smiled.

"I can look after myself, except when strange men gallop over me without any warning!"

"How could I have imagined in a million years," Roydon Sanford asked, "that the long grass would be concealing a woman, and a gypsy at that?"

"I suppose if I really had been a gypsy and you had trampled on me, it would not have mattered."

"I see you did not miss *Madame* Porquier's dislike of the gypsies," he said. "It is understandable. At times they can be very difficult in this part of the world when so many of them come to Saintes Maries de la Mer."

He paused.

"But they are colourful, and the ceremony in the sea, which is derived from an age-old polytheistic religion, is very impressive."

He saw that Valda was interested and went on:

"Once a year the *Rom,* or gypsies, in the fifteenth century took on their shoulders the statue of Ishtari and waded into the sea as an act to promote fertility."

"I did not know that," Valda said.

"The gypsies keep their Festival very much to themselves," Roydon Sanford went on. "But you can understand that the farmers find them a nuisance not only on their way to Saintes Maries but also on their way back."

He smiled as he said:

"For the past week all the roads converging on the Camargue have been packed with a steady stream of gypsies in caravans of every size, shape, and age."

"I understand that most land-owners are hospitable to the gypsies," Valda said, "and allow them to camp for the night or longer if necessary."

"It is not the land-owners who suffer from the gyp-

sies," Roydon Sanford replied, "but the farmers.
Chickens mysteriously disappear, even lambs evade the
watchful eye of the shepherd."

He laughed as he went on:

"French parents resent the money their daughters
pay to the fortune-tellers and their sons expend on
games of chance and all the other paraphernalia by
which the gypsies going to Saintes Maries de la Mer will
extract every possible franc from the simple peasants."

"I do not think you know the gypsies as well as I
do," Valda said sharply. "They are not the rogues you
think they are! If they take something to eat as they
pass, who shall blame them? This is a rich country and
they are very poor. It is difficult for any of us to understand why the good things of life are so unevenly dis-
tributed."

Roydon Sanford laughed.

"I can see," he said, "you are one of these new wom-
en who are demanding the vote!"

"Do I sound like a Suffragette?" Valda asked. "Perhaps I shall become one."

"You certainly do not look like one. But I will tell
you what you do look like."

There was a note in his voice which made her glance
at him sharply.

"On second thought," he said, "I will keep the compliment I was about to pay you until we know each
other better."

He turned away from the window as he spoke and
Valda realised he had heard *Madame* Porquier at the
door. He crossed the room to open it for her.

She carried in a tray on which reposed a large coffee-
pot and two big cups.

There was a dish on which Valda saw a pile of hot
meat pasties. There was thick cream for the coffee
and as *Madame* put the tray down on the table Valda
decided she was after all quite hungry.

"You will feel better, *M'mselle*," *Madame* Porquier
said, "when you have had something to eat and drink.
Having an accident, however small, is always upset-
ting."

"Thank you," Valda replied. "I am very grateful."

"It is a pleasure," *Madame* Porquier replied as she went from the room.

"I can quite see," Valda said as she poured out the coffee, "that if I stay here long I shall get as fat as *Madame!*"

"Perhaps that is why I work." Roydon Sanford smiled. "There is nothing like riding to shake down a meal, however large."

"Do you think I could ride tomorrow?" Valda asked.

"I will speak to *Monsieur* when he comes in this evening," Roydon Sanford replied. "I am sure he will let you have one of his horses, although they are in short supply at the moment because the mares are foaling."

"Are you speaking of the Camargue horses?" Valda asked quickly.

"I am," he answered. "Both wild and tame."

"Then I must take pictures of their foals," Valda cried. "I would like above all things to photograph the foals soon after they are born."

"As you can imagine, it is not easy," Roydon Sanford answered. "Not only are the mares nervous, but also the stallions who keep guard over them can be very difficult with strangers."

He saw the disappointment in Valda's face and said:

"At the same time, I promise you I will do my best to see that this Photographic Exhibition of yours is a success, and I do agree that pictures of the foals would be a great attraction."

"Then can we try tomorrow?" Valda asked excitedly.

"If that will please you," he answered. "In the meantime you can take some pictures of the foals on the farm. There are quite a number of them."

Valda ate one of the meat pasties and realised Mr. Sanford had been right in saying they were delicious.

She then drank her coffee, adding a little more cream to cool it, and said:

"I am ready! Can we go and see the foals?"

Roydon Sanford rose to his feet.

"I am sure your pictures will be a success," he said.

"You bring a vitality to everything you do and everything you say. If you can transmit that to a photograph, it will be sensational!"

"That is what I thought about the Exhibition I saw in London," she said. "There were some beach scenes that were fantastically real."

"I think we must have visited the same Exhibition!" Roydon Sanford said. "Were there also some pictures taken at night of the Houses of Parliament?"

"There were!" Valda said. "I see you know they were by Paul Martin."

"So that is why you have become a photographer!" Roydon Sanford remarked. "I must admit I was tempted myself, but I was too lazy to make the effort."

"What do you do when you are not here on holiday?" Valda asked.

She was walking towards the door as she spoke.

"I have done a great many things in my life," Roydon Sanford answered. "In fact I am the proverbial rolling stone. I have been, this past month, examining the different wines in the Rhône District for a friend who is thinking of importing them."

"That is most interesting."

But Valda was in fact intent on finding her camera, which had been left in the kitchen.

It was standing on a side-table near where Roydon Sanford had been sitting when she had brought her wet clothes down to *Madame* Porquier.

She picked it up now, felt the leather case, and decided that he was right in thinking it was unlikely that the water on which it had been floating had penetrated the thickness of the leather.

"I inspected the box carefully," Roydon Sanford told her, "and even if it had been wet, by the time we got here it was quite dry."

"Then I think we will risk the film that is already in it," Valda said, "because it is a new one."

She did not add that she had not changed a film for so long that she was slightly uncertain as to how to do it.

When the time came she was determined to be alone and read the instructions carefully.

"Let us go and see the foals," Roydon Sanford suggested. "Do you want a hat?"

"I did not bring one with me," Valda answered.

"You are certainly travelling very light," he said with a smile, "and in the circumstances, your gypsy costume must have been useful."

"Especially when I was with the gypsies," Valda added without thinking.

"You have been with the gypsies?"

She heard the astonishment in his voice and thought perhaps she had been indiscreet. Then she told herself it had nothing to do with him.

"I am very fond of the gypsies," she said almost defiantly, "and the ones who brought me to the Camargue were old friends. I cannot think why you should be so suspicious of them."

"I am not," Roydon Sanford answered. "I am only astonished at the way you move about by yourself. Surely with your looks you must at times find yourself in—shall we say, an uncomfortable situation?"

"Only when I am taken by surprise, like this afternoon," Valda retorted.

"I was not referring to that sort of situation," he said gravely.

"As I have told you, I can look after myself," Valda replied. "I think it is a good thing for women to be independent, to make their own minds up about what they want to do."

"And what do you want?"

Valda thought for a moment, then she said:

"I want to be free . . . free of restrictions, of being confined or ordered about."

"But that is the fate of all young women," Roydon Sanford argued. "First they must submit to parental authority, then they must be looked after by their husbands."

"Why should they be?" Valda asked. "Besides, who wants a husband? There are enough men in the world so that one does not have to marry the first one who comes along."

She was thinking of the Marquis d'Artigny as she spoke, and she told herself that although he might be her Stepfather's first choice, it was very unlikely that his second or third would be any more acceptable.

Roydon Sanford did not speak, and carrying her camera Valda said as she opened the door into the yard:

"Do let us hurry! If we do not start to take my pictures soon the sun will be going down, and unlike Paul Martin I am sure I shall be no use with a camera at night!"

They spent what to Valda was an entrancing two hours photographing the foals in a field only a short distance from the farm-house.

Although the white horses were tame and in frequent use, as soon as Valda and Roydon Sanford appeared the stallions threw up their heads and eyed them with suspicion.

Many of the mares were still in foal, the others had their young beside them, and for the first time Valda learnt that the foals were not born white.

Most of them had a thick black woolly coat with a white patch on their foreheads. There was an occasional rust-coloured or fawn one.

"In about eight months," Roydon Sanford explained, "they will lose their youthful coat, and by the time they are about four years old their colouring will have changed to pale grey. Subsequently it turns finally to white."

Valda started to take her photographs.

The white horses silhouetted against the trees bordering the field or the buildings with their red roofs had a natural elegance which she felt must somehow convey itself to the film.

"They are beautiful!" she kept saying as she took picture after picture. "So beautiful I feel I shall never admire any other breed of horse, however magnificent it may be!"

"Wait until you see them wild," Roydon Sanford said. "Tomorrow I will take you to a place where I know the mares are foaling. We must be careful not to disturb them and be very wary of the stallions."

"They can be dangerous?" Valda asked.

"As dangerous as a Camargue bull!"

"I must photograph them!"

"We will certainly try," he promised, and Valda felt he was amused at her enthusiasm.

She only ceased taking photographs when the sun had lost its strength and the trees were throwing such long shadows that she was afraid the photographs would be too dark.

They walked back to the farm and Roydon Sanford said:

"We eat early in the *Mas*. In fact the guardians come in from the farm at sunset and we must have our meal at the same time."

"But of course," Valda said. "I would not like to up-set *Madame* when she has been so kind as to have me here."

When they entered the kitchen it was to be assailed with the most delicious smell of cooking. On the table Valda saw an enormous collection of vegetables besides truffles, a variety of mushrooms, asparagus, and olives, which she knew from experience, because they came from Provence, they were the best in the world.

"Despite the meat pastie I am hungry, *Madame*," Roydon Sanford remarked.

"You have not worked very hard today, *Monsieur*," *Madame* Porquier said severely. "I am not certain you deserve a big supper!"

"You must blame *Mademoiselle* for my short-comings," Roydon Sanford said. "I was on the way to join *Monsieur* when she prevented me from going any further."

"That is a most unfair accusation!" Valda said. "*Madame* would be right if she starved you as a punishment!"

She smiled at him as she spoke and he realised she had two dimples, one in each cheek. Then she ran up-stairs to her bed-room, determined to put her camera in a safe place.

She reckoned she must have taken at least twenty-five photographs, perhaps more.

'I must keep plenty of film for the flamingos and the wild horses,' she thought. 'And some for the gypsies in Saintes Maries de la Mer.'

There were two more rolls of film and out of all the snapshots she took she hoped there would eventually be forty or fifty worth showing in an Exhibition.

She was now absolutely convinced that she would have one in Paris and that her Stepfather and all his friends would be amazed at her accomplishment.

As she took off her afternoon-gown Valda thought how lucky she was to have found this delightful *Mas* in which she could stay.

She was not so ignorant as not to realise that a village Inn could be extremely uncomfortable. Also vaguely she thought that there might be unforeseen dangers from the type of men who frequented it.

Valda was, however, very inexperienced about the world—in fact she was completely innocent.

She had no comprehension of what life could be like outside the luxurious, cossetted existence which had been hers ever since she was old enough to think.

It was quite an experience even to have to undress herself without a servant to help her, and to do up the gown she had brought with her to wear in the evening.

It had, she thought, been an exceedingly good choice.

Made of fine muslin, inset with rows of Valencian lace, it was light as a piece of thistledown and quite uncrushable.

It was draped over the bodice in a manner which accentuated the smallness of her waist, and because she had been careful not to bring anything which might appear too dressy, while ner neck and shoulders were bare, the gown had long tight sleeves of the same lace, fastening at the wrist.

The skirt was full and swept out over a silk petticoat which, rolled up tightly, had taken up very little room in the linen bag.

Thinking her ordinary slippers would be too heavy, Valda had put in a pair of heel-less satin ones which made her appear smaller than usual, but which had certainly weighed little more than an ounce or two.

She had no idea as she changed that her gown would have caused a sensation in any way-side Inn, and certainly would be considered shocking by the ordinary peasant, who had never seen a woman in evening-dress.

Even Roydon Sanford looked slightly surprised when she walked gracefully into the Salon where he was waiting for her.

He too had changed, but not into evening-clothes.

Instead he wore a velvet coat which Valda had always associated with artists, and an unstarched shirt, although his collar was stiff.

"You look very elegant!" he said as Valda approached him. "And, may I add, extremely beautiful!"

Valda's eyes widened in surprise at the compliment.

She had a feeling it was too familiar, and yet at the same time the fact that he obviously admired her appearance made her feel a little warm glow inside.

Looking at him, she realised that he was far betterlooking than he had appeared in the rough clothes he had worn in the afternoon, and without the sombrero which all the guardians wore.

His hair grew back from a square forehead and his features were clear-cut without being particularly outstanding.

It was his grey eyes that were the most arresting thing about him.

There was, Valda decided, a challenge in them, yet at the same time they were uncannily perceptive.

They reminded her vaguely of her father's, who always appeared to be searching for something which he could not find.

But where her father's eyes had a hardness which came from his strong determination and an inflexible will, Roydon Sanford's eyes twinkled as if he was amused by life and slightly cynical about it.

The same, Valda thought, might apply to his mouth.

It was a firm mouth. But when he smiled there was a twist to his lips which was disconcerting.

She could not explain it to herself, except that it

gave her a feeling of uncertainty and at the same time made her shy.

She did not answer what he had said. She merely sat down on one of the hard chairs with its mahogany frame, and looked up at him questioningly.

"How could I have imagined when I rose this morning," he said, "and breakfasted with the Porquiers, that I should find myself this evening dining in state with a very lovely woman?"

"I was thinking as I changed," Valda said, "that I was fortunate to have met you. I am sure that you can show me parts of the Camargue that I might never have found on my own."

"I can indeed," Roydon Sanford answered. "Moreover, if you wandered about the Camargue alone you might encounter real dangers from the quick-sands."

"The quick-sands?" Valda echoed. "I had no idea there were any!"

"The *sables mouvements,* as the French call them, of the Camargue are a very real deterrent to keep strangers away," Roydon Sanford answered. "The ground looks the same everywhere, but here and there where it is crusted it conceals a natural well of mud and water of anything from a few to twenty feet deep!"

"How frightening!" Valda exclaimed. "But how do the cattle and horses avoid them?"

"They do often get lost in them," Roydon Sanford answered, "which is why the guardians keep a sharp eye on them. Everyone will tell you stories of how dangerous it is to walk alone into the marshes."

"I am glad you warned me," Valda said. "That is exactly what I had intended to do."

"The *sables mouvements* are not the only danger you might meet from being alone," he said.

Valda looked up at him and smiled.

"I have a feeling you are going to lecture me," she said. "I shall not listen, so do not waste your breath!"

"Somebody ought to talk to you—and very seriously!"

"As I have already told you, I can look after myself!" Valda answered. "And I want to be free!"

She paused and he asked after a moment:

"What are you looking for?"

The question took Valda by surprise. Then because he had spoken seriously she answered him lightly and with a frivolous note in her voice:

"Excitement . . . adventure, and perhaps . . . love! Why not?"

"Of course," Roydon Sanford agreed. "Why not?"

Chapter Five

Riding beside Roydon Sanford, Valda thought she had never been so happy.

It was early in the morning and the air was crisp and clear; the sky, deep blue and infinitely high, promised a hot Summer's day.

They had been riding for half an hour and the colour of the flowers and the butterflies fluttering above them was breathtaking.

Yellow flags lined the banks of the irrigation ditches and the shallow edges of fresh-water swamps.

Some of the ponds were covered with the delicate star-shaped blossoms of the wild buttercup, the dainty tamerisks were a warm pink, and swarming over them were thousands of yellow, red, and brown dragonflies.

"Everything that has happened since I left home has been an enchantment," Valda told herself.

Last night having dinner alone with Roydon Sanford, she had enjoyed it as she had never enjoyed a meal before.

She felt a little shy as they sat down at the table, wondering how she should amuse and interest him and suddenly feeling inexperienced and very young.

But as the delicious food was put in front of them by *Madame* Porquier and they both started to eat hungrily, the barriers seemed to disappear and there was so much to say, so much to discuss.

They started the meal with the asparagus which was growing in long beds outside the farm, and to follow there was young lamb cooked with herbs and garnished with mushrooms, small green paprikas, and courgettes which had a special flavour.

To drink there was a famous Rhône wine which Roydon Sanford told Valda he had brought with him from the vineyards and which tasted like bottled sunshine.

The dinner ended with a local cheese and fruits in a wicker basket which had been picked only a few hours earlier, and Valda felt as if they had only just begun their conversation.

There was so much more to say, but despite her interests she could not help feeling a sudden sleepiness creep over her.

It might have been in part due to the Rhône wine, but as her eye-lids drooped a little Roydon Sanford exclaimed:

"You are tired! You have had a long day and must go to bed. If we are to go riding and try to take photographs of the foals and the flamingos, you will need to be up early."

"I was awake soon after four o'clock this morning," Valda told him almost apologetically. "The gypsies were on the road by five."

"Then you have every excuse to be sleepy," he smiled, "and I need not attribute it to the boringness of my conversation!"

"It is certainly not that!" she answered. "I have never enjoyed a dinner more, especially as this is the first time . . ."

She was about to say this was the first time she had ever dined alone with a man, but she felt that would be too revealing. He might ask her questions she would find difficulty in answering.

She knew from what he had said earlier that he was in fact suspicious that she should be travelling alone and unchaperoned.

She thought that only by reiterating constantly that she liked her independence and wished to be free would he really believe her to be one of the modern young women about whom a great deal of criticism was voiced in the newspapers of both France and England.

"First time for what?" he asked.

"First time in a Provençal *Mas*," she replied.

As she spoke she rose from the table and he said:

"Good-night, Valda, and sleep well. There are many things to do tomorrow."

She put out her hand but, instead of shaking it, to her surprise he kissed it.

She told herself that he had adopted French manners and although she felt that she should rebuke him for calling her by her Christian name, it would, she thought, be more in keeping with her pose of independence to expect it.

She had fallen asleep the moment her head touched the pillow and she awoke in the morning to hear *Madame* Porquier pull back the curtains.

"I would have let you sleep on, *M'mselle*," *Madame* Porquier remarked as Valda gazed at her hazily, wondering for a moment where she was, "but *Monsieur* Sanford asked me to inform you that he will have the horses outside in half an hour, and your breakfast will be ready in fifteen minutes."

"Horses!" Valda exclaimed, and jumped out of bed.

She came downstairs dressed in her thin leaf-green riding-habit just as *Madame* Porquier carried a large breakfast and steaming-hot coffee from the kitchen into the Salon.

She was followed by Roydon Sanford and Valda's eyes were shining as she exclaimed:

"You have persuaded *Monsieur* to let me have a horse?"

"I have a young mare for you," he replied. "She is rather skittish, but you assured me you are an experienced rider."

"You shall see for yourself!" Valda replied.

They both ate a large breakfast, then with Roydon carrying the camera they went out to the yard to find that for Valda there was an attractive roan-coloured animal on which there was a side-saddle.

"Thank you," Valda said as Roydon lifted her onto it with his two hands on each side of her waist as he had lifted her the day before.

Her mount was in fact rather skittish to start with, but they galloped over the grass-lands near the farm until, as Roydon said: "The monkey has gone out of her!"

Then they turned towards the *étangs* and the swamps where it was wise to go slowly, and Valda had a chance to see the birds.

A dozen herons rose from their nests, chattering as they made their way along a narrow, partially clear path through a reed-thicket.

There was the whistle of the marsh-harrier, the squeak of the wild-rails, the ringing of the bearded tits, then unexpectedly several hundred yards away in the middle of some shallow water Valda saw a mass of pink and white.

She reined in her horse to stare at the flamingos with delight.

She could hardly believe that their glorious pink plumage was not a mirage.

Then as she realised that they were too far away for her to photograph them, they rose into the air and she heard their desolate unmusical cry.

They moved away, then changing direction, their leader a little ahead, they flew over Valda and Roydon so low that they could see the rose-red of their legs and under-wings—a brilliant flash of colour in the morning sun!

One moment they were there, the next they were gone, and Valda cried despairingly:

"I did not have a chance to take a picture of them!"

"You will see others," Roydon promised consolingly. "I was not expecting them to be here. If we do not find them during the day, I know a place where they always seem to be in the evening just before the sun sets."

"There are lots of them?" Valda asked, her disappointment abating a little at his words.

"Monsieur Porquier tells me that no less than twenty thousand come to the *étangs* at this time of the year."

"I must have a photograph of them!"

"You will, I promise you," he said. "In the meantime, let us find the mares. Perhaps you might also take some pictures of the white egrets or the colourful *guepier.*"

"That means a bee-eater, does it not?" Valda asked.

"That is right," he answered. "And occasionally we see parrots here and even the Egyptian ibis, which is thought to be an infallible sign of dry weather."

"It is so exciting!" Valda exclaimed with a little sigh of contentment.

They rode on and now the reeds were massed almost like a jungle, and as they moved through them the birds were rising all the time, protesting noisily at their intrusion.

It was very beautiful with clumps of tamarisk and occasionally trees, and everywhere brilliant flowers and creepers, many of which Valda had never seen before.

Roydon Sanford drew in his horse.

"We have to walk from here."

"Walk?" Valda questioned in surprise.

"That is why I insisted on your borrowing a pair of boots from *Madame* Porquier," he answered. "This is the place from which to approach what I call the heart of the Camargue."

Looking down at the soft, marshy ground where the water gurgled beneath the horses hoofs, Valda realised that he had in fact been very sensible in insisting that she wear a pair of rubber boots.

Madame Porquier told her they had belonged to her daughter who was now married and had left the *Mas*.

They were a little large for Valda, but as she dismounted she was glad that she had not to walk, as she had yesterday, bare-footed.

There were twigs on the ground which would have been painful, besides the fact that she was not really anxious to feel the muddy frog-infested waters squelching between her toes.

Roydon took the horses' bridles and tied the two animals skilfully to eash side of a large fallen tree.

There was grass they could crop and Valda was sure it would be impossible for them to escape.

Having made certain they were securely tied, Roydon came to her side and took her arm.

"Now walk slowly and quietly," he said. "We must

not talk, otherwise the horses I hope to find on the other side will hear us coming."

He spoke in a low voice and she smiled as they started to move through the thicket.

It would have been impossible to go quickly as the thorny shoots of the smilax caught Valda's full skirts and the creepers seemed to be deliberately pulling at her hair to prevent her from going any further.

They walked a little way. Then without any warning, directly ahead of them there was a sound of violent thrashing about, reed stems snapping, water splashing! There was a grunting and snorting which seemed to echo all round them.

Then like the devil himself with his infernal cohorts, a pack of wild boars burst from a hidden lair and ran straight past Valda.

With their bristling black coarse hides, their tusks, and their small evil eyes, they seemed to her to be creatures from hell, and instinctively she turned towards Roydon for protection.

He put his arms round her and half turned his back towards the boars.

It was all over in a matter of seconds. Only a huge black sow, the last to burst from the bullrushes, hesitated for a moment as if she might attack the intruders.

Valda felt Roydon stiffen against her; then the sow was gone and they could hear the herd snorting away in the distance.

She drew a deep breath and realised she was trembling. Without thinking, she hid her face against his shoulder.

His arms were very comforting.

"It is all right," he said. "The boars seldom attack a man unless they have been taken by surprise."

"I . . . I was frightened!" Valda murmured, her voice unsteady. She raised her head as she spoke and found that his mouth was only a few inches from hers.

Just for a moment they looked at each other, then his lips took possession of her.

She was too astonished to move. But when she would have pushed him away it was impossible.

His lips were hard and possessive and it flashed through Valda's mind that being kissed was not as exciting as she had thought it would be.

Even at the thought, a strange flame seemed to flicker in her breasts and up into her throat.

It was a wonder that she had never known. An excitement which was like an arrow passing through her —painful, and yet, as it moved, becoming an ecstasy that was indescribable.

She felt her lips quiver beneath his and now his mouth seemed more demanding, more possessive, and she felt as if she melted into him and the beauty of the Camargue was part of him too.

Her whole being vibrated as if to a note of music, and she knew vaguely that this was what she had longed for, this was what she had wanted.

Time stood still: it might have been a century or a few seconds before he raised his head and her lips were free.

She looked up at him, unable to move, unable to speak, only aware that her whole body was pulsating with a wild rapture which was indescribable.

"You are very sweet," Roydon said, and his voice was deep.

She wanted to answer him, but her voice seemed to have died in her throat.

He smiled at her and it was the smile a man might have made to a child as he said:

"We must go! There is a lot of work for us to do!"

Valda could not reply, she only knew that she had no wish to go anywhere. She only wanted to stay where she was—in his arms.

She wanted him to go on kissing her, to evoke within her that marvellous feeling which still seemed to be throbbing within her breasts.

It had swept away not only her will but also her mind.

Carrying her camera, Roydon turned and walked ahead, as if to protect her from any other danger which might appear, and Valda could do nothing but follow.

She found herself moving as if in a dream, unable to

think of anything except that she had been kissed. It was more wonderful, more exciting than anything she had ever anticipated.

They reached the end of the thicket and reeds and Roydon stopped to stand very still.

He put his hand out behind him, took hold of Valda's arm, and pulled her gently forward to where peering through the leaves she could see a stretch of dry grass and on it a herd of about thirty horses.

With the mares were a number of foals, some of them making their first tentative, unsteady steps on long, spindly legs.

The foals with their black woolly coats and the white patch on their foreheads made an exquisite picture against the white coats of their mothers.

Moving his arm very carefully and slowly, Roydon handed Valda the camera.

She took it from him and for a moment it was difficult to remember how to handle the camera or that she really was interested in photography.

All she could think of was the pressure of his lips on hers and the breathless excitement which still seemed to linger in her throat.

Then because he expected it, she focussed the Kodak on the herd and as she did so the stallions and several of the mares, as if they sensed danger, became restless.

They raised their heads, their nostrils flared, their ears pricked up.

Valda could see their muscles twitching under their gleaming white coats. Necks were taut, legs were pressed firmly against the ground.

As their sense of danger became more acute, Valda felt they were ready to gallop wildly away and she might never see them again.

Hastily she began to take her photographs.

She remembered that Roydon had said the stallions could be dangerous, and there was one magnificent animal who seemed to be looking straight towards them as if he knew the very direction from which danger might come.

She took picture after picture. Then without saying a word Roydon took the camera from her and she knew he thought they had been there long enough.

There was no doubt that as she continued to photograph them the herd was becoming increasingly nervous.

Walking with the utmost care, Roydon led the way back through the thicket and tamarisk bushes, passing the place where they had been frightened by the wild boars.

Now there was nothing more frightening than the white-and-yellow blossom of the rock roses, the wild gladioli, and the tall slim stems of asphodel which the ancient Greeks believed covered the plains of the underworld.

A few seconds later they stepped back into the sunshine and found the horses they had tied to the fallen tree.

Valda looked up at Roydon as he turned to smile at her.

"Thank . . . you," she said, and wondered to herself if she was thanking him for showing her the wild horses or for the wonder of his kiss.

They rode on and it seemed to Valda as if the beauty of the land round them was even more breathtaking than it had been before.

A delicate pale-blue haze against a rich green marked a patch of wild rosemary, and she felt as if she saw it not only with her eyes but also with her heart.

The brilliantly coloured butterflies winging their way through the air and the glittering wings of the bees and bumble-bees were part of the magic inside herself.

Now Roydon led her away from the *étangs* to the dunes, and as they galloped over them there was a view of the distant sea, vividly blue in the heat of the sun, as the Madonna's robe.

In front of them, stretching to the horizon, there was a variegated pattern of water, salicornia, and brightly glistening expanses of dry mud.

Looking back, the hilly ranges of the Alpilles could be seen.

It was all so lovely, and when Roydon drew in his

horse they stood still, watching the air shimmering above the hot sand.

"I wanted you to see this," he said. "It is a complete contrast to where we went early this morning, but it is still essentially the Camargue!"

"It is very beautiful!" Valda exclaimed.

"And so are you!" he replied.

His eyes were on her lips and she felt as if he kissed her again.

Then he turned the horses and she knew he was taking her home.

Though they moved at a good steady speed, they had come a long way and it was getting very hot when finally the *Mas* came into sight.

"What about the flamingos?" Valda asked.

"I think you have done enough for the moment," he answered, "and you should rest this afternoon. I will take you out at about half past five. There is a place not far away where the flamingos can be found if we are lucky."

"It would be difficult to photograph them without good sunlight."

"There will be enough."

Valda had the feeling that they were saying one thing with their lips and something quite different with their hearts, and yet she could not be sure of it.

She only knew that something strange and thrilling had happened to her since they had set out that morning, which was as wild and wonderful as the Camargue itself.

Did Roydon feel the same?

She was not certain, and once again she felt very young and inexperienced.

They reached the *Mas*. Roydon helped Valda down from her horse and before entering the kitchen she took off her muddy boots which *Madame* Porquier had lent her.

Madame was busy at her stove and turned to say with a smile:

"You are very late, *M'mselle*. I was beginning to think you would not want any luncheon."

"I am ravenously hungry, *Madame!*"

"Then it is a good thing I kept your meal warm for you," *Madame* replied. "It will be on the table as soon as you have washed."

Valda ran upstairs. Before she even took off the jacket of her habit she looked at herself in the mirror.

She almost expected that her face might have changed.

But her large blue eyes, as they looked back at her, seemed very little different from normal, save they were shining as brightly as the sunshine on the *étangs* and her mouth was as soft and pink as the tamarisk blossoms.

"I want him to kiss me again," she told herself, and blushed because it sounded so immodest.

* * *

The next time she looked in the mirror it was too dark to see her reflection.

The sun was sinking in a blaze of crimson glory and they had come back to the farm after photographing the flamingos.

They had seemed unbelievably beautiful as they flew in from the Mediterranean islands.

The sun had lost its power and Valda was a little apprehensive as to whether the photographs would be as good as she wanted.

There had been about a hundred flamingos and she wondered if in fact any photograph could do justice, in its prosaic black and white, to such a colourful spectacle.

'Only a painter,' she thought, 'could portray the birds with their long curved beaks, the fascinating rose colour beneath their wings, and their long scaly red legs.'

Roydon had taken her as near as possible to them over the hard-packed salt flats, and the flamingos stood almost at attention, eyes like guardsmen's as they warily watched their approach.

Then after Valda had taken perhaps a dozen photographs, as if at some secret signal they rose in unison.

Falling in line behind their leader, honking their peculiar unmelodious cry, they swept upwards into the sky and swooped in a semi-circle to land on another *étang* far away in the distance.

'Perhaps one photograph will be really good,' Valda thought.

Then with a little lilt to her heart she remembered that there was always tomorrow.

Roydon would take her riding again.

She would tell him she was not satisfied and also that she wished to photograph the Camargue bulls in addition.

There was nothing unusual about them: they were to be seen in every part of Provence and her Stepfather had a herd of them. But they would prove an excuse for her to be with Roydon.

'And besides,' she thought, 'there are all the other birds of which he has spoken.'

The thought of spending days at the *Mas* in his company made Valda think again as she changed for dinner that it was an enchanted place.

She had always expected to find romance in a Castle or in some great Château, connecting them in her mind with the mediaeval Knights whom she had thought must personify all that represented love.

But Roydon was not a Knight, although he had come to her in the guise of a guardian, carrying his trident as if it were a lance and mounted on the leather saddle which had borne crusading Knights to fight for Jerusalem.

She thought of how he had kissed her in the thicket and she felt herself quiver again with the wonder of it.

As she finished dressing she wished she had another gown to wear rather than the one she had worn last night. She wanted him to admire her. She wanted to see a glint in his eyes when she appeared.

As she entered the Salon her eyes were blue in her small face and the dark red of her hair caught the last dying gleam of the sun sinking behind the plane trees.

Roydon had been standing at the window and as he

turned towards her he was silhouetted against the glory of the sky and she felt as if he came to her in a blaze of fire.

They looked at each other and she felt her heart begin to thump in a strange manner within her breast and the breath come quickly between her lips.

"I was thinking what a happy day we have had together," he said.

"It has been very . . . happy for . . . me," Valda answered rather breathlessly. "The happiest day I have . . . ever known."

"Do you mean that?" he asked.

Because the expression in his eyes made her feel shy she looked away from him into the garden.

"It was . . . enchanted!" she said softly.

"That is what I thought," he replied. "Just as you have enchanted me!"

Valda waited for him to say more, but he turned his head towards the door and once again she realised that he had heard *Madame* Porquier approach with a tray.

The table was laid and like last night there were two candles in the centre of it. After she had brought in the first course, *Madame* Porquier lit the oil-lamp which cast a golden glow and took away the stiffness from the room.

The food was as good as the night before, but Valda had no idea what she was eating.

She was only acutely conscious of the man beside her, aware of the strength and largeness of him as she had never been before, or perhaps it was just his masculinity.

She kept telling herself that she must be careful that he should not guess what she was feeling lest he should realise how strange this was to her. How all that had happened since they met was different from anything she had imagined was possible.

"I must talk," Valda told herself, and yet it was difficult to find words.

When she met his eyes she felt something quiver within her, and she knew it was part of the same feeling that he had evoked when he had kissed her in what he had said was "the heart of the Camargue."

"You are not feeling so tired tonight?" he asked as they were finishing dinner.

"I am not in the least tired!" Valda answered. "You made me rest this afternoon, something I never do when I am at home."

"What do you do when you are at home?" Roydon asked. "And where is home—in Paris?"

"Most of the time," Valda answered.

"Do you walk about Paris alone as you do here?" he asked.

There was a pause before Valda replied:

"Why not? But I am often with . . . friends."

"Male or female?"

"When I am walking, if that is what interests you . . . male."

She was thinking of her Stepfather as she spoke and how, because the Comte insisted on taking exercise, they would walk in the Tuilleries Gardens, along the banks of the Seine, or sometimes even as far as the Bois.

Her mother much preferred driving and Valda liked to ride, but the Comte was insistent that walking was essential for good health.

When they were not in the country Valda would accompany him, and found, as he anticipated, that she returned home with glowing cheeks and a sense of well-being.

They rose from the table to move, almost as if it was an instinctive need within them both, towards the open window.

Darkness had fallen while they were at dinner, and now there was only a faint translucent glow in the West and the stars were coming out one by one overhead.

It was very quiet save for the occasional note of a bird late in going to roost.

Below them was the rustle of some small animal creeping through the undergrowth, but otherwise there was only a deep silence like a suddenly suspended melody from a violin.

Then from the cypress trees came the sound of the nightingales, singing in perfect harmony softly fluting passages alternating with brash metallic ones, plaintive tones with those that were lyrically soft.

It was so enchanting, so unexpected, that without thought, without even realising what she was doing, Valda turned towards Roydon.

His arms were waiting for her, and as he drew her close she felt herself quiver and it was part of the music of the birds.

His mouth came down on hers and she could no longer hear anything but the music within her own heart.

He kissed her until the stars seemed to fall from the sky and glitter at their feet. Then he held her closer still and she felt as if he made her his so that she no longer had any individuality of her own but was a part of him.

He took his lips from hers to kiss her eyes, her cheeks, her small nose, then again her lips.

Now she throbbed and quivered and felt as if he had awakened a flame within her so wild, so wonderful, that it was part of the magic of the Camargue; at the same time, it was her soul and she must give it to him.

Once again he raised his head and now he said in a voice with a deep note in it she had not heard before:

"Go up to bed, my darling."

He turned her round as he spoke and she did as she was told because for the moment it was impossible to think and quite impossible to speak.

Obediently she crossed the Salon without looking back and went up the stairs to her bed-room.

Madame Porquier had turned down the bed, and there was one candle alight on a side-table.

Valda undid her gown and hung it up in the wardrobe. Then she took off her petticoats and her other clothes and laid them on a chair and put on her night-gown.

She sat down at the dressing-table to take the pins from her hair and let it fall like a dark cloud over her shoulders.

She brushed it automatically, hardly aware of what she was doing.

Every nerve and every instinct in her body was concentrating on the wonder she had felt when she had been kissed.

She almost felt as if Roydon's lips were still on hers and she could feel his touch on her eyes and on her cheeks.

"This is love!" Valda told herself.

She looked in the mirror and saw, as she expected, that she did in fact look quite different.

Her eyes had a radiance. There was something almost spiritual about it.

She stared at herself for several minutes, then she gave a deep sigh of happiness and wonder, and got into bed.

She heard footsteps coming up the stairs and knew it was Roydon going to his room, just opposite hers.

"Tomorrow we will talk," Valda told herself. "I will tell him that I love him."

She thought that he had been right in sending her away so that the rapture of the kiss he had given her in the garden would not be spoilt.

To have to speak after what she had felt would have been too banal, too commonplace. They had touched the height of bliss.

"He understands," she told herself, "as I never thought any man would . . . understand."

How could she have known that in coming to the Camargue, and trying to prove to her Stepfather she was capable of looking after herself, she would find the one thing she wanted?

A man who loved her and whom she loved.

She shut her eyes at the very wonder of it.

Here was someone who did not know of her wealth and therefore could not be influenced by it. Here was someone to whom she was a nobody—a girl trying to earn her own living by taking photographs.

It was everything she believed possible, and yet had been afraid she would never find.

It was love! It was romance! It was perfect, as pure

and noble as the love which had been sung and extolled by the Troubadours who had lived in the Courts of Love.

"I am so lucky . . . so very lucky!" Valda told herself, and remembered she had not said her prayers.

She sat up in bed, clasped her hands together, and shut her eyes.

"Thank You . . . God, thank . . . You," she whispered, and found there was no need to say any more.

Her whole being was uplifted in an inexpressible gratitude for the blessing she had received from Heaven.

Her eyes were still shut when the door opened and she looked in surprise to see Roydon enter the room.

He was wearing a long robe which reached to the floor and the frill of his night-shirt was white against the darkness of his chin.

He shut the door. Then as Valda still stared at him in astonishment he walked towards the bed.

The look in his eyes made her feel shy and there was a twist to his lips that had something cynical about it.

She stared up at him, her eyes very wide and questioning as he stood looking down at her.

In the big square wooden bed with its heavy curtains, she seemed somehow small and insubstantial silhouetted against the white linen pillows.

"That is how I thought you would look with your hair loose," he said in his deep voice. "But it is longer than I expected."

With an effort Valda stammered:

"W-what do y-you . . . want? I do not . . . t-think you s-should . . . come into my bed-room."

"You were not expecting me?"

"No . . . of course . . . not!"

"But you knew that we had not finished saying goodnight to each other?"

She looked at him and her fingers trembled as they moved instinctively as if to cover her breasts.

Her night-gown was fastened at the neck and extended to her wrists with a little frill that fell over her hands; but it was made of the very finest lawn and trimmed with lace, and even in the dim light of one candle it was easy to see the curve of her rose-tipped breasts.

"You should not . . . come in . . . here," Valda said, and her voice was low and a little frightened.

"Are you playing with me?" Roydon asked in an amused tone.

He sat down on the side of the bed and instinctively Valda pushed herself back against the pillows behind her.

"You are very lovely, very alluring, very desirable," Roydon said, "and I think in the exceptional circumstances in which we find ourselves, we can accelerate matters."

His smile was somehow more cynical as he went on:

"I see you expect me to woo you, to wait a little longer before we reach together what we know is inevitable. But, darling, why should we waste time? I knew when I kissed you what we both wanted, and there is no need for pretence."

"I do not . . . understand," Valda said. "I only . . . know that it is . . . wrong for you to come into my . . . bed-room."

"Wrong?"

Roydon repeated the word with raised eye-brows.

"Yes, wrong!" Valda answered. "I know my . . . mother would think it . . . wrong that I let you . . . kiss me, though it did not seem to me . . . wrong, only very . . . wonderful. But this . . . I think this is . . . different!"

"What are you trying to say to me?" Roydon enquired.

"I am . . . saying," Valda answered, "that . . . gentlemen do not . . . come into ladies' . . . bed-rooms."

She thought as she spoke that what she had said sounded ridiculous.

Of course she knew from the conversations she had listened to about her mother's friends that gentlemen did go into ladies' bed-rooms.

She did not know what they did, but presumably it was to "make love."

Did the French ever talk of anything else?

"I . . . I think what I . . . mean," she said hastily, "is that you should not come to . . . my . . . bed-room."

"I thought you liked me," Roydon said.

"But I do!" Valda replied quickly. "I like you more than I have ever liked anyone before! But however much we like each other . . . it would not be . . . right for you to be . . . here when we are . . . alone."

"Listen, my sweet," Roydon said. "I quite understand what you are trying to say to me. But, my dear, you have made it quite clear what sort of life you lead, and, as I have already said, I find you very desirable and I think perhaps you are not entirely indifferent to me."

He smiled as he went on:

"Why should we go through all the conventional preliminaries of pretending that you must be modest and maidenly, when inevitably, after all the initial skirmishes are over, we shall love each other as nature intended?"

As he spoke he bent forward and put his arms round Valda, drawing her close against him as his lips sought hers.

She felt that tremor of excitement go through her that she had felt before. It was like a dagger piercing her body with a warm tide of wonder rising into her throat.

Then with an effort she tried to push him from her.

"No, no!" she cried. "Please . . . no!"

There was a note in her voice that made him pause. Then she said:

"I am . . . frightened . . . I do not . . . understand what you want to . . . do, but I . . . know it would not be . . . right!"

"What do you not understand?"

He had not taken his arms from her but now his lips were no longer seeking hers.

There was a silence, then Valda turned her head to hide it against his shoulder.

"I may be . . . wrong," she said in a whisper, "but I think . . . perhaps . . . you want to . . . 'make love' to me, and I do not . . . know exactly what that . . . means."

She felt him stiffen. Then he moved and, putting his fingers under her chin, turned her face up to his.

"What do you mean—you do not understand?"

Her eyes flickered because she knew he meant her to look up at him.

Then as if he compelled them to do so, her eyes met his.

"No-one has . . . explained it to me," she said. "I have . . . heard people talking about . . . 'making love' but I feel . . . inside me that unless one is . . . married it must . . . really be a sin!"

For a long moment Roydon stared down at her. Then he set her free, taking his other arm from round her.

"I think you have a lot of explaining to do, Valda," he said quietly. "And I want to know the truth."

There was a silence so intense that Valda could hear her own breathing. Then she said, a tremor in her voice:

"What . . . do you want . . . to know?"

"Exactly what you are doing here alone," he replied, "dressed as a gypsy and telling me you are living a free life of your own."

There was another silence. After a moment he said: "I am waiting!"

Valda did not look at him. Her eye-lashes were very dark and long against the whiteness of her cheeks.

"It is . . . not your . . . business!"

"You made it my business when you let me kiss you this morning."

"I could not . . . help it."

"But you thought it was wonderful—that is what you said just now."

"It was . . . wonderful! I did not know a . . . kiss could be like . . . that."

"How many men have kissed you?"

"None . . . except you!"

"You expect me to believe that?"

"It . . . is the . . . truth," Valda said in a very small voice.

She thought as she spoke that she was being very stupid.

He was worming her secrets out of her, and yet he was so masterful, so authoritative that it was impossible to defy him.

"And what about these other men? The men you do not wish to marry? The men with whom you have walked in Paris?"

Valda did not answer and after a moment he said:

"I intend to learn the truth, Valda, if I sit here all night. The alternative, of course, is to let me make love to you as I intended to do when I came into this room."

"But . . . why? Why should you . . . want to do . . . that?"

"It is not a question of why I should want to," Roydon said with a smile. "It is what any man would want who was alone with anyone as lovely as you. But you gave the impression of being very experienced and sophisticated. Are you really telling me, on your sacred word of honour, that you have never had a lover?"

"No . . . of course . . . I have not!" Valda said in a shocked voice.

"How old are you?"

The question took her by surprise.

For a moment the answer trembled on her lips. Then resolutely, as she bit back the words, Roydon reached out and holding her chin turned her face up to his.

"Tell me the truth!" he said. "I am not prepared to listen to any more lies!"

She tried to twist her chin away from him but he would not let her go.

"The truth!" he insisted.

"I . . . am . . . e-eighteen."

"It is what I might have known. And I suppose you have run away from home?"

"Y-yes!"

"Why?"

"Because my Stepfather . . . wished me to . . . marry

a man I have never seen . . . a marriage that would be arranged . . . as is . . . usual in . . . France."

Valda's voice died away. Then as Roydon did not speak she went on:

"I wanted to prove to him that I could take care of myself so that he would believe that I was capable also of choosing the man who would be my husband."

"And you thought out this wild escapade on your own?"

Valda nodded.

"Have you any idea how crazily—how irresponsibly you are behaving?" Roydon asked.

There was a note of anger in his voice which annoyed her.

"I am doing what I want to do!" she flashed. "And when I do go home, having looked after myself and bringing back the pictures I have taken of the Camargue, my Stepfather is bound to realise he is . . . wrong."

"Do you really think you will have proved that you can look after yourself? Do you think that is what you are doing at this moment?"

She looked at him wide-eyed.

"Supposing," he said slowly, "I pay no attention to your objections! Supposing I get into bed with you at this moment and make love to you! What could you do about it?"

It flashed through Valda's mind that it might be rather wonderful, as wonderful as his kisses when they had been in the thicket and in the garden.

Then she said:

"I do not . . . think you will do . . . that. You know I . . . believe it to be . . . wrong."

"I may listen to you," Roydon said, "but a great many men would pay no attention, whatever you might say."

"But I have not . . . met them!" Valda retorted.

"That is more by luck than by good judgement!" he said, and there was still the note of anger in his voice. "The whole thing is ridiculous! Tomorrow I shall take you home."

"I will not go with you!" Valda cried. "I am not going home, and you cannot make me! After all, you do
not know where I live, and you have no right to order
me about!"

"And suppose I give myself the right?"

He reached out his arms as he spoke and put them
round Valda again.

"If I made love to you, Valda, with or without your
consent, would not that automatically authorise me to
look after and protect you from other men?"

Chapter Six

He drew her closer as he spoke and Valda tried to push him away.

"No! . . . No! . . . No!"

Her voice was lost as he tipped her back against the pillows and his lips were on hers.

He kissed her fiercely and roughly with a violence which was frightening.

She was still struggling, but ineffectively, and she realised how weak and helpless she was against his strength.

His lips hurt her, she was conscious of the pain of them, and for a moment she felt panic-stricken, feeling herself captured and overpowered.

Then, just as had happened before, the dagger-like pain which swept through her body turned into a rapture and an ecstasy.

The fight went from her and she became soft and yielding, her body moving against his, her whole being bemused by a wonder which seeped into her throat and up to her lips.

Her will was gone, even her thought of self.

Once again she was part of him, but now it was more wonderful, more glorious than it had been before, and she felt as if the small flame which had flickered in her breasts burst into a blazing fire which utterly consumed her.

She could only feel to a point of intensity when she could no longer think.

The fire within her seemed to leap higher and Valda knew that her body was aching for something she did not understand, but which she was willing to give him because she was already his.

Time, space, the whole world vanished, and he carried her into a Paradise where they were alone—no longer human but part of the Divine.

Then when a century of ecstasy had passed, Roydon raised his head and her lips were free.

For a moment she was unable to move and it was impossible to breathe.

"I love . . . you! I love . . . you!"

The words came from the depths of her soul.

"My darling, this is madness!"

"It is . . . perfect! It is . . . Heaven! Please . . . kiss me . . . again."

Roydon looked down at her and his mouth was very close to hers. Her red hair was streaming over the pillow and over his arm.

In the light from the candle he could see her lips warm and trembling from his kisses, her eyes wide and shining with a passion she had never known before and did not understand.

For a long, long moment he looked at her until with an effort he took his arms from her and rose from the bed.

"I told you that this is madness!"

"W-why?"

"Because you must not love me. It is something which cannot happen."

"But . . . it has . . . happened!"

Roydon walked across the room to the window to pull back the curtains as if he was in need of air.

He stood with his back to the room and Valda watched him, the happiness fading a little from her face and a feeling of uncertainty replacing the throbbing glory within her breasts.

"What . . . is . . . wrong?" she asked after a moment.

"Everything is wrong!" he answered. "And that is why you have to forget that I kissed you."

"W-why? Oh, why?"

Valda pushed herself up in the bed, raising her head from the pillows against which he had crushed her.

"Tomorrow," Roydon said in a hard voice, "you will leave—or I will! On one thing I am determined, we cannot stay here together!"

"But why . . . not?" Valda cried. "What have I . . . done? What have I . . . said that has . . . upset you?"

He did not speak and she said:

"Was it . . . because I . . . said I . . . loved you?"

There was something lost and pathetic in her voice. He turned from the window.

"No, of course not," he replied. "I am only trying to convince myself it is not true."

"But it is true," Valda insisted. "You are all that I have . . . wanted and . . . longed for . . . the man I felt existed . . . somewhere in the world if only I . . . could find . . . him."

"You are not to say such things to me."

Their eyes met across the room, then abruptly Roydon turned once again to the window.

"I do not . . . understand," Valda said. "Are you trying to tell me that you do not . . . like me, or . . . perhaps I have . . . shocked you?"

As if he could not help himself, a smile came to Roydon's lips and he walked back to the bed.

"You have not shocked me, my sweet. I am only upset that you should take such risks with yourself and behave in such a dangerous manner."

The light came back into Valda's eyes.

"Then we can be . . . together?"

"No!"

The monosyllable seemed to echo round the room. The darkness was back in Roydon's expression and the harsh note in his voice.

"I have to think for you," he said. "If you are sensible, you will go back to your Stepfather and do as he wishes."

"I . . . cannot! I cannot do . . . that! Especially now that I have . . . met you."

"I can mean nothing to you," Roydon said, "and that is why I intend to say good-bye to you now, at this very moment! As you have pointed out, I have no right to interfere in your life, or what you wish to do with it. So you can stay here or join your friends in Saintes Maries de la Mer. I shall leave first thing in the morning."

"No! No! You . . . cannot do . . . that!" Valda cried desperately. "Stay . . . please stay . . . if only for one more . . . day?"

"And one more night?" Roydon asked. "Do you believe I could kiss you again as I did just now and not make you mine?"

Their eyes met and she saw the fire in his.

They looked at each other until Valda said in a vioice he could hardly hear:

"That is . . . what I want . . . to belong to you . . . to be yours. . . ."

His lips tightened. Then he said:

"You do not understand what you are saying."

"I think . . . I do," Valda answered slowly. "I love you, and . . . if you 'made love' to me as you wanted to do . . . I should belong to you . . . completely . . . and I know now it would be the most . . . marvellous . . . perfect thing that could . . . happen to . . . me."

"And afterwards?" Roydon asked sharply.

"Afterwards?" she repeated in a puzzled voice.

"There is always an afterwards," he said roughly, "when you would go your way and I would go mine."

She looked at him but she did not speak, and after a moment he said:

"I cannot marry you. Let me make that quite clear."

Valda was very still. Then in a voice which hardly seemed her own she asked:

"Are you . . . married . . . already?"

"No," he answered, "but I cannot marry anyone. I cannot afford to do so!"

There was a silence which was almost suffocating.

"If you . . . could," Valda asked at length, "would you . . . would you marry . . . me?"

There was a pause before he answered:

"The question does not arise, so there is no point in answering it."

"Why can . . . you not marry . . . anyone?"

Roydon rose to his feet.

"I have said there is nothing to discuss," he

answered. "I am going to bed, Valda, and we will say good-bye now, while I can do so."

Instinctively she put out her hands towards him as he stood looking at her face in the candlelight.

"For God's sake," he ejaculated harshly, "do not look at me like that! I am doing what is right and some-day you will understand."

"Please ... please ..." Valda said.

"I can stand no more," he answered, and turning walked from the room, shutting the door sharply behind him.

She heard the door of his room slam and to her it sounded the knell of doom.

"He has gone!" she told herself. "He will never come back and everything that is worthwhile in life . . . everything I wanted . . . everything that is beautiful . . . has gone with him."

She thought despairingly that never again would she know real happiness, the ecstasy she had felt when he had first kissed her amongst the reeds and the wonder and rapture that had been theirs under the stars.

Now with this last kiss, when he had started roughly, almost brutally, to hurt her, he had lit a fire which had swept through them both to evoke something wild and glorious.

She knew, although he would not say so, that Roydon had felt as she had.

He too had been swept away by a kiss so perfect that there were no words in which to express it.

And now he had gone!

It seemed to Valda that he had left only a darkness behind him, a darkness which left her utterly depleted of everything in which she had faith.

He had also taken away hope.

As if a voice told her so, she knew that she would never find a love again as she loved now.

This was the supreme wonder, a love which was both spiritual and physical. A love which every man and woman sought but so few found.

She had found it, but it had already gone and there would be no return.

Despairingly she thought of what lay ahead.

She would go back to Merlimont. She would no longer fight against her Stepfather's plans for her, because whatever man he chose as her husband, she could never be anything but a card-board figure of a wife!

A wife who no longer possessed either her heart or her soul, because they had been given to somebody else.

She thought of the years stretching ahead of her, years of emptiness, years bereft of Roydon.

It was, Valda thought, like being suddenly struck blind and knowing that never again would one see the sunshine and the flowers, the sky or the sea.

There would be darkness. A darkness that was not only in one's eyes, but also in one's heart.

'I cannot bear it!' she thought. 'I cannot live like that!'

Hardly aware of what she was doing, she got out of bed and walked across the floor.

Very quietly she opened her door.

Standing just outside on the landing, she listened.

There was no sound from Roydon's room and no light beneath his door.

'He is asleep,' she thought. 'I mean so little to him, after all that has happened, that he can leave me and . . . sleep! He will go away in the morning and I shall be alone . . . alone for the rest of my life!'

For one moment she contemplated going into his room to plead with him, on her knees, to love her if only for a little while. Then she knew it would be hopeless.

He had made up his mind, she had heard it in the steely determination in his voice, she had known it by the way in which he had left the room.

Nothing she could say would change it.

Slowly, walking almost silently on her bare feet, Valda went downstairs.

She could see the way from the light shining through the open door of her bed-room.

Below, the door of the Salon was open and as she

entered it she saw there was a faint radiance from the uncurtained window at the far end.

The window was open and she realised that Roydon must have left it unlatched when he had come upstairs after sending her to bed.

Valda crossed the room and stepping outside stood in the same place where Roydon had kissed her after they had heard the nightingales.

The birds were still singing, but now they intensified the despair within her to the point where it became unbearable, an agony like a physical wound, and yet even more hurtful.

She looked up and felt that the stars, twinkling against the velvet of the sky, mocked her, like the song of the birds.

How could she ever look at beauty again when Roydon was not there to share it with her?

How could she live without his arms round her, his lips on hers?

Blindly, miserably, driven by a despair to escape not from the *Mas* but from herself, she moved away from the house, walking almost like a sleep-walker.

She passed the cypress trees and turned towards the sea.

A salt wind lifted her hair against her forehead and seemed to draw her in the right direction.

Vaguely somewhere at the back of her mind Valda remembered Roydon speaking of the dangers of the quick-sands, of the bulls, and of the white stallions.

It was danger, she thought, that she was seeking, a danger that might obliterate the agony within her, bringing relief from her unhappiness and her fear of the future.

She walked on. Now the ground was damp; moths touched her face with their soft wings and flew away, and sometimes her feet sank into the mud.

The hem of her night-gown was soaked: it did not seem to matter.

She only knew she could not go back and that oblivion lay ahead.

'I will go to the sea,' she thought. 'I will swim out into it and go on swimming.'

A heavy, sweetly astringent fragrance hung on the air. The perfume of thyme and rosemary, of lavender and rock-roses.

The starry sky was stretched out over the sleeping land, but the night was filled with sound.

There was the croak of tree-frogs, the hollow hoot of an owl, the high squeak of bats.

Valda was unaware of anything but the misery which encompassed her like a cloud.

Vaguely she saw large, massive, shadowy figures ahead and there was the pungent smell of sleeping animals.

The *taureaux* had settled down for the night and were dozing. Only the twitching of ears, the flicking of tails, and muted snorts proclaimed their presence.

She moved past them, her white night-gown standing out against the darkness. The ground now was harder and there was grass beneath her bare feet.

Suddenly she was aware of a noise behind her which signified danger!

A Camargue bull was driving her away from his herd.

She could hear not only his pounding hoofs but also the noise of his breathing. She knew he would be carrying his head low, muscles strained in his desire to attack an enemy with his deadly, dagger-like horns.

She had no chance of escape; she would be gored, tossed, and probably killed.

She screamed in terror but the sound was lost as she ran frantically—quicker than she had ever run in her life.

"Help! Help!"

The cry was strangled in her breathlessness and she was desperate that no-one would hear her.

Then as the hoofs were thundering just behind her, with every nerve in her body alert to the thrust of the horns, she found herself falling forward and screaming again.

She hit water violently and was blinded by the splash of it.

She expected to sink but found instead that she was on her hands and knees in what she realised after a stunned moment was an irrigation canal. It was several feet deep but, since the weather was dry, only partially full.

Above her on the bank she could hear the bull snorting and pawing the ground, ready to give battle.

She had eluded him, and as she did not move, he thought her poor sport and moved away, still blowing a protest through his wide nostrils at her intrusion.

Slowly and with difficulty Valda stood up.

The front of her night-gown was soaked, but that was of no consequence. She must go on. The sea was still ahead.

She climbed up the further side of the canal to stand, feeling weak and faint, and curiously disembodied.

Overhead there was the protracted fluting of the stone-curlew; bats flitted against the stars.

The wind swept away her faintness and she moved on, dragging her legs as if they were crippled.

The ground was damp. Another slip and her feet were in water. She thought she must have walked into an *étang*.

"The sea . . . I must get to sea," she told herself.

The water grew deeper and it was cold.

Valda paused; she was too exhausted, she wanted to lie down; only the thought of the sea kept her moving forward.

There was a sound behind her of splashing water, and she thought in a panic that the bull must still be following her.

She half-turned, terrified that in the deeper water she would be unable to run. Then Roydon's arms were round her and she was close against his chest.

"My darling! What are you doing? Where are you going?" he asked, and the words seemed to tumble over one another.

The relief at seeing him made it impossible to reply,

and as if he understood what she was feeling he picked her up in his arms.

The water from her wet night-gown dripped down into the stillness of the *étang*.

He waded back through the shallow waters onto the firm grass and she hid her face against his shoulder. She was in his arms, she was safe! Safe as she had thought she would never feel again.

"How could you have been so crazy as to walk through the herd?" he asked.

His tone was not angry, only deep with some emotion she could not understand.

"I saw what was happening and thought the bull would toss you," he went on. "I could only try to reach you from another direction."

His voice was breathless and she could feel his heart pounding and knew he must have been running to reach her.

Valda shut her eyes.

His arms held her, they were together. Nothing else mattered. She was close to him again.

"Where were you going?" Roydon asked.

"To the . . . sea," she whispered.

He asked her no more questions, but carried her back towards the *Mas*. Surprisingly, by the way he went it was not as far as she had walked alone.

Valda thought that once she felt him kiss her hair, and yet she was not sure.

Only when they reached the farm and he had carried her in through the window of the Salon and up the stairs did she open her eyes and raise her head from his shoulder.

He carried her to the threshold of her room, then he put her down on the floor.

"Have you another night-gown?" he asked.

For a moment the question seemed hardly to make any sense, until as she knew he was waiting for her reply she managed:

"Y-yes."

"Put it on and get into bed."

He had not taken his arms from her, but now as he would have done so she clung to him.

"Please . . . do not leave . . . me."

"I am going to talk to you," he said gravely, "but as I do not wish you to catch cold, you must do as I tell you. I am going downstairs to get us both a drink."

Still her hands were clinging to the lapels of his robe, and he said gently, as if reassuring a child:

"I will come back—I promise!"

She turned away with a little sigh. He shut the door and she heard him going downstairs.

She had brought two night-gowns with her. She took off the one she was wearing, which was soaked and stained by the weeds in the canal, and left it in a heap on the floor.

She dried herself with a towel, drew from a drawer the other night-gown, and having put it on crept into bed.

She was now trembling violently, not only owing to the cold but also because of the reaction from the intensity of the emotions which had made her behave as she had.

She could understand Roydon thinking her crazy, and yet it had seemed the only thing she could do to drown the pain and misery within herself.

It was a little time before she heard him coming back upstairs, and when he entered the room she saw that he carried a tray in his hands on which there was a pot of coffee, two cups, and a small glass.

He set the tray down on the bed beside her, and picking up the glass he held it out to her.

"Drink this, it will save you from catching a chill."

"What . . . is it?"

"Brandy."

She took the glass from him, sipped it, and wrinkled her nose as the fiery liquor seared her throat.

"All of it!" Roydon commanded.

She obeyed him and he said:

"Pour out the coffee while I change."

For the first time she realised that he had followed

after her still wearing the robe in which he had come to her bed-room.

It was wet where he had waded after her into the *étang*, and she imagined that the night-shirt he wore under it was wet too.

He went to his room and she poured out the coffee. Already the brandy had stopped her trembling, but she still felt cold and started to take tiny sips from one of the cups.

Roydon came back to her in a few minutes in a white shirt and a pair of trousers he had fastened round his waist with a belt. He wore no tie but instead there was a coloured handkerchief tied like a scarf inside the collar of his shirt.

It gave him a somewhat raffish appearance, and she thought as he came towards her that no other man could be so attractive.

Her love made her feel weak and helpless, and she watched as he lifted the tray to put it on the floor, and taking the cup of coffee she had poured out for him, drank it.

Then he sat down on the bed.

Now Valda looked at him a little apprehensively, expecting him to be angry.

For what seemed to her a long time his eyes rested on her pale face and worried eyes. He seemed to be studying her.

But his silence seemed ominous and at last Valda could bear it no longer. The tears gathered in her eyes.

"I . . . I am . . . sorry."

The words were only a murmur, but as she spoke them the tears ran down her cheeks.

"I am . . . sorry . . . please . . . please . . . do not be angry with . . . me."

"I am not angry, I am trying to understand."

"I . . . had to go . . . I could not bear the pain . . . of losing . . . you . . . I wanted to . . . forget and I . . . thought . . . "

Tears choked her.

"What did you think?"

"That . . . if I was in . . . d-danger . . . I would not

. . . mind . . . anymore . . . I wanted . . . to be . . . hurt
. . . but when the bull . . . chased me . . . I ran . . .
away."

Her voice faltered; her tears were blinding her. Roydon drew a white linen hankerchief from his pocket
and wiped her eyes.

Because he was gentle it made her cry more bitterly.

"Can you really love me so much?" he asked.

"There is . . . nothing in the . . . world but . . . you."

"Are you sure?"

"More . . . sure than I have ever been of . . . anything in my . . . whole life!"

"You are very young."

"I do not think that . . . age has anything to do with
. . . love. I know now that a person may live to be a
hundred and never find it . . . when it comes, there is
. . . nothing to discuss . . . nothing to say . . . it is there
and one knows that it is real and very . . . very wonderful!"

Roydon drew a deep breath and said:

"I understand what you are saying to me—how
could I not understand when I feel the same? But I
have to make you realise how little I have to offer
you."

Looking at her with an expression in his eyes which
seemed to her to be hard and almost indifferent, he
said:

"I am a man with no money, no roots, and, at the
moment, no future!"

"That does not matter to . . . me."

"You have to know what you would be taking on,"
he answered.

She wanted to put out her hands towards him, to
draw him nearer to her, but she knew he was determined not to touch her until she had heard him out.
She waited.

Her eyes were very large in her small face but her
heart began to thump wildly.

He was here, she was near to him. She no longer had
to reach the sea.

"I told you that I was a rolling stone," Roydon

went on. "When I was twenty-one I quarrelled with
my father, who was a very truculent man, and went my
own way, determined not to be beholden to him."

His voice was low but emotionless as he went on:

"I travelled all over the world, earning my living in
many different ways. I have been a lumberjack in Canada, I have bought and sold furs in Alaska. I went to
the East to see what I could do by trading, and had
quite a fair amount of success."

He paused as if he was thinking back into the past
before he went on:

"I moved round, and as I grew older I spent what I
earned on further travels and enjoying myself. I had no
wish to settle down and there was no point in my doing so."

Listening to him, Valda thought that when he had
spoken of "enjoying himself," that enjoyment must
have involved women, and she felt a sharp stab of
jealousy.

He did not expect her to comment and continued:

"I had seven years of this sort of life. Then I returned home a year ago because I had learnt that my
father was dead and my mother very ill. She was in
fact worse than I had expected."

Now there was a note of pain in his voice and Valda
thought he must have loved his mother deeply.

"I brought back a certain amount of money with
me, and I found it was urgently required for opera-
tions, for Nursing-Homes, and such luxuries as had
been denied my mother during my father's lifetime."

"Did she live?" Valda asked.

Roydon shook his head.

"She died two months ago," he answered. "By that
time I had spent all the money I had saved and I owe a
considerable amount more."

"I am sorry you . . . lost her," Valda said in a soft
voice.

"She was suffering and she wanted to die," Roydon
replied. "But I was able to be with her to the end, and
that mattered more than anything else."

He spoke simply. Then as if he did not want to linger on the unhappiness of what had happened he said:

"I therefore had to get work and get it quickly. That is why I took the job in France a friend offered me of tasting and advising on new wines for import into England. The job is not highly paid but it is enjoyable, and, as I have worked very hard, I came here for a short holiday before returning home to find something else to do."

He looked at Valda. Then turned his eyes away from her to stare at the candle.

"Now do you understand why I said I could not marry you or anyone else?" he asked. "I can hardly keep myself, let alone a wife!"

Valda drew in her breath.

"Do you . . . want me?"

"You know I want you!" Roydon replied. "Like you, I realise that what we have both felt is something magical and very wonderful. Something which to me has never happened before and may never happen again."

There was a note in his voice which made her feel as if she vibrated to it.

"You are what I have always longed for, and looked for all over the world, only to be disappointed until—now."

"Do you . . . mean . . . that?" Valda asked breathlessly.

"I mean it!" he answered. "But, my darling, how can we possibly get married when all I can offer you is a life of poverty and privation?"

"Do you suppose I would mind if I could be with . . . you?" Valda asked. "And anyway . . . I have . . . some money of my . . . own."

Roydon smiled.

"Enough, I suspect," he said, "for you to buy the films for your camera! But whatever you may possess, you do not suppose I would allow my wife to keep me?"

He spoke lightly, but Valda knew without being told that he was intensely proud and to him the knowledge that she was rich would be a positive deterrent, not an asset.

"At least we would not . . . starve," she said.

"We would not do that anyway," he answered sharply. "I am not completely nit-witted. I can always make some money one way or another, as I have done in the past. But would it be enough for you, my darling?"

Before she could answer he went on:

"There might be moments when we could not live in any comfort, when we might have to travel to strange parts of the world, but not in de-luxe cabins or by Express trains."

"Do you really think such things would matter?" Valda asked.

"I would not mind for myself," he answered, "but you have never known poverty. You have never been forced to economise over your gowns, your food, or the type of roof over your head at night."

"All I want is to be with . . . you," Valda said.

"I have a feeling that what I long to do is wrong," Roydon continued, "certainly wrong from your point of view, and perhaps eventually even from mine. Supposing the time comes when you reproach me? Supposing when you are older you do not think the sacrifice of what you have given up and what you have endured is compensated for by our love?"

Valda's eyes lit up in a smile and she held her arms out to him.

"Do you really believe that love like ours could ever be wrong?" she asked.

Just for a moment he hesitated, then he bent forward and her arms were round his neck.

She pulled his head down to hers but he did not kiss her.

Instead he put his cheek against hers and held her closely so that she could feel his heart beating.

"I am trying to be sensible," he said. "I am trying to think for both of us; but you make it very difficult for me, my sweet."

"There is nothing to think about," Valda answered. "All I want is to be with you. I do not care if we have to live in a hovel or sleep under the stars, so long as I can be with you. We were meant for each other . . . it is fate. Nothing . . . anyone can say or do can prevent us from belonging to . . . each other."

There was a little tremor of fear in her voice because she was thinking of her Stepfather.

"Can we be married at once?" she asked. "Tomorrow or the next day? Then, when I am your wife, I can introduce you to my mother and Stepfather."

"Is that what you want?" Roydon asked.

"Yes," she answered. "Please . . . please let us do that."

She knew before he spoke that he was not going to agree.

"No, darling," he answered. "That would be taking an unfair advantage of your youth and inexperience. I have to meet your mother and talk to your Stepfather, who is, I imagine, your Guardian."

"Let us get married . . . first," Valda begged.

"I think that would be cowardly," he said. "I am sure the reason you are in such a hurry is that you are afraid they will disapprove."

Valda did not answer, but he felt her tremble and added:

"I promise you, my precious, that because I want to marry you much more than you want to marry me, I shall be very persuasive."

Valda thought despairingly that he had no idea of what lay ahead.

She could imagine how violently her Stepfather would disapprove of her marrying a man who had no money of his own, and although Roydon was obviously an English gentleman he had little else to recommend him.

Almost as if she could foresee the future, Valda could hear him refusing to listen and turning Roydon away from the Château.

She still had her arms round his neck.

"Please let us be married at once," she pleaded. "I am afraid that something might separate us. You might leave me as you did just now and I should never see you again."

"You have convinced me that I cannot ever do that," Roydon answered. "How could you have done anything so foolhardy—so wicked—as to go off by yourself? You might have wandered into the quick-sands, and you only just escaped being gored!"

She did not reply and after a moment he said:

"I could not believe, when I heard you go downstairs, that you would go out alone into the night."

He felt Valda quiver against him and he said quietly:

"You have not yet told me why you were going to the sea."

"I just wanted to swim away from . . . everything," Valda whispered. "I could not . . . face the future without . . . you."

His arms tightened round her until it was painful.

"My foolish, ridiculous darling!"

He moved to kiss first her forehead, then her eyes, still wet from her tears, then very gently her mouth.

There was this time no passion or fire in his kiss, but a tenderness that somehow made Valda feel as if she wanted to cry again.

"You have been through enough for tonight," he said tenderly. "I want you to go to sleep, my sweetheart, and we will talk about everything tomorrow."

"You will not go . . . away? I will not wake up to find you have . . . left?"

"I will never leave you," he answered. "You are right, Valda, we belong to each other and I intend to look after you and love you for the rest of our lives. Does that make you happy?"

She drew in a deep breath.

"You know it does," she answered. "I love you! I love you, and if you are not with me I have no wish to go on . . . living."

"I shall be very angry if you talk like that," he said. "At the same time, I feel as you do, that it was fate, my precious, for us to find each other."

He smiled. Then he said:

"It is also the magic of the Camargue. The magic which holds us both spellbound so that we can never escape."

"I could never . . . wish to do so," Valda said against his lips.

He kissed her gently, then released her arms from his neck and rose from the bed.

He pulled the sheets up to tuck them beneath her chin.

"Good-night, my darling little love. The future is in the lap of the gods, and the gods have been kind up to now."

"I am sure they will help us."

He looked down at her, at the happiness in her eyes, at her red hair and the softness of her mouth.

"I love you!" he said.

Then he blew out the light.

Alone in the darkness, Valda felt an irresistible happiness sweep over her.

This is what she wanted. This is what she had prayed for. She knew that nothing mattered, nothing was important, except her love for Roydon and his for her.

At the same time, she knew there were enormous difficulties ahead, of which he was not aware but which to herself she could not deny or belittle.

Because Roydon loved her she felt she held a precious jewel in her hands and it was hers.

Yet she had to admit not only was there the danger of her Stepfather trying to take it away from her, there was also the problem of Roydon himself.

He did not have to tell her that he was proud and that he was not the type of man who would live on his wife's money.

She knew it was an intrinsic part of his make-up, and that everything in his character and personality would revolt at the thought of having an immensely rich wife while he himself had no means.

She knew too that there would have been a fascination and in a way a special happiness in enduring the kind of poverty he had envisaged for them together.

She would have to make ends meet when there were hard times, she would have to economise on her clothes, buy cheaper food, put up with uncomfortable surroundings.

But none of it would matter because she was doing it for love, for a man who would fill her whole existence.

This situation, of course, need never arise when there was her wealth at their disposal. Yet she knew Roydon would resent every penny of hers that he must spend, simply because he had nothing to give in return.

He would not think that love was enough, even though she would be prepared to sacrifice every penny she had in return for one kiss.

How could she make him understand? How could she explain?

It seemed to Valda as if all the difficulties and problems were like an armed enemy standing between her and her happiness.

Then she told herself that no problem was insurmountable.

How could she have believed a month ago that she would find herself here in the Camargue, in the room next to the man she loved, with a chance of becoming his wife?

That would have seemed an improbable dream, and yet it had come true. So why should she be so faint-hearted about what lay ahead?

And yet the answer was that running away from the Château, reaching the Camargue, and even finding Roydon had been her decision, not his.

Now she was concerned with his feelings, his pride and his happiness. That made everything different.

It was then that Valda covered her face with her hands and began to pray. Prayer had brought her safely to where she was now and prayer must help her in the future.

"Help me, God. Please help me!" she prayed. "There must be a way in which I can marry Roydon and make him happy . . . despite my money. I cannot fail now!"

She prayed so intensely that she half-expected to hear the answer in her mind or perhaps in her heart!

But there was only silence and she wondered desperately what solution tomorrow could bring.

Chapter Seven

Valda was already up and half-dressed when *Madame* Porquier came to call her.

"Monsieur has asked me to tell you, *M'mselle,"* she said, "that you will be riding to Arles today, so you must wear your riding-habit."

"Riding to Arles?" Valda exclaimed in delight, knowing this meant that she would see more of the Camargue.

"Oui, M'mselle. Monsieur spoke to my husband, and as he has two horses that he intended to sell to a friend who has wanted them for some time, it is convenient that you and *Monsieur* should take them to him."

"What a good idea!" Valda agreed.

Madame Porquier put the cup of coffee she had brought Valda on the dressing-table.

"You have not much to pack, *M'mselle,"* she said, looking at the brown linen bag which was nearly full.

"No, indeed," Valda answered. "I brought very little with me, as you know."

"It will be a long ride," *Madame* Porquier suggested reflectively, "and you have no hat. I was wondering if you would like me to lend you a straw hat that my daughter wore when she was here last Summer. It has ribbons which tie under the chin."

"That would be very kind of you," Valda said. "I am afraid it will be very hot and my mother gets annoyed if I burn my skin."

"I should feel the same, *M'mselle,* for your skin is white and very beautiful."

"Thank you, *Madame."* Valda smiled.

Madame went from the room and returned a little later, when Valda was dressed, with a straw hat which she recognised as the type worn by the young girls of Provence when working in the fields.

Made of coarse straw, with a wide brim and ribbons which tied under Valda's chin, it was very becoming.

"Thank you very much," she exclaimed, "and I will leave it with your friends in Arles."

"If you will do that, *M'mselle*, when my husband next goes to market he will collect it and bring it back here in case my daughter requires it again."

"I am very grateful," Valda said.

Having tried on the hat, she took it off and went downstairs. Her blue habit, as vividly blue as her eyes, made her look to Roydon as if she had just dropped from the sky.

He was in the Salon and as she entered she stood for a moment looking at him. It seemed to her there was no need to put into words how much she loved him. He must be aware of it.

As he held out his arms she ran towards him and he held her close and kissed her.

"You look happy, my darling," he said.

"I am happy," she answered. "I only wish we had not to leave today."

"I have made arrangements, as *Madame* has undoubtedly told you, that we will ride to Arles," Roydon said. "That will give us many more hours in the Camargue."

"And many more hours with . . . you!" Valda said softly.

He kissed her again, then said:

"It is in fact the easiest and most comfortable way to journey to Arles. When we reach there, how far will it be to your home?"

"Less then five miles," Valda replied.

"Then what we will do is hire a carriage to carry you to your mother and Stepfather," Roydon said. "I will follow later."

Valda was about to protest, then she thought he was wise.

It would be better for her to arrive home alone, so that after her Stepfather had shown either pleasure or anger—she was not certain which—at seeing her, she could tell him and her mother about Roydon.

She wished, however, that he could be with her, because already she was feeling apprehensive of what their reaction would be when she told them she intended to marry a man she had chosen for herself.

Roydon was watching her face, and as if he sensed what she was feeling he said:

"We have to face the fact, my darling, that your Stepfather may insist on a long engagement, or make us wait at least until I have found a house where we can live and a job so that I can maintain us."

Valda drew in her breath.

"Is that going to be difficult?"

"Not really," he replied. "I have been thinking about it in the night. I know of one firm with whom I dealt when I was in the East, who would be only too glad to have me. They have already made me an offer, as it happens, but I refused them, as I did not wish to live in London."

"And now you do not mind?" Valda asked.

"I would live in hell itself if it meant that I could be with you!" he answered.

She would have moved back into his arms had not *Madame* Porquier at that moment brought in their breakfast and set it down on the table.

"All your favourite dishes this morning, *Monsieur,*" she said to Roydon. "I would not wish you to leave me hungry!"

He laughed.

"As always, *Madame,* I shall leave you a good deal heavier in weight than when I arrived!"

Madame Porquier turned to Valda.

"When you have finished your breakfast, *M'mselle,* my husband would like to say good-bye to you."

"I could meet him now," Valda said quickly. "I would not wish to keep him from the fields."

"There is no reason to hurry, *M'mselle,*" *Madame* Porquier replied. "He has the horses to finish grooming

and many last-minute instructions that he wishes to give
to *Monsieur*. He will wait."

She bustled away and Valda sat down at the table.

There were quite a number of dishes over and above
what had been served the previous morning.

"I have left my clothes in Arles," Roydon remarked
as if he was following the train of his own thoughts.

"Your clothes?" Valda questioned.

"I do not think your relatives would be very impressed with me as I appear at the moment," he answered with a smile. "I will come to meet them looking,
I promise you, very much more prepossessing and, I
hope, responsible!"

"I think you look handsome whatever you wear,"
Valda said impulsively.

Then as he raised his eye-brows she blushed and
added:

"That sounds very . . . forward. I spoke without . . .
thinking."

"I am flattered!" he said. "And may I tell you in
return that you look very lovely today, lovelier, I
think, than you have ever looked! But then they tell me
that love is a great beautifier!"

She blushed again and felt shy at the deep note in his
voice.

When they had finished breakfast they went outside
and Valda took photographs of *Monsieur* Porquier and
Madame, and the horses, and several of the *Mas* itself.

"I will send you copies," she promised. "And also of
the pictures we took yesterday of the wild horses and
the flamingos."

"We shall treasure them, *M'mselle,*" *Madame* Porquier said, "and when you come back you shall see
them in my album."

"I hope very much I shall be coming back," Valda
answered.

Her linen bag was fastened behind the high saddle
on one horse and Roydon's clothes, which were rolled up
in what appeared to be a light blanket, were attached
behind the other.

Only the camera seemed likely to be somewhat of an

encumbrance, until Roydon managed to fix it rather skilfully in the leather pouch on the front of his saddle. These were made for carrying the small items of guardian equipment.

Then with many expressions of goodwill they said good-bye to the Porquiers and rode away from the yard.

To Valda's surprise, on leaving the *Mas* they turned away from the road which led over the Étang de Vaccarès and went instead directly Northwards.

She looked at him for explanation and he said:

"I wanted you to see some more of the Camargue before we leave. You will even have a glimpse a little later of the plains of the Crau on the other side of the Rhône."

"I should like that," Valda said. "I have seen it in the distance from the ramparts of the Citadel at Les Baux."

"Then you know it is flat and desolate?" Roydon asked.

"That is what it looks like!" Valda replied.

"The Crau is a very strange place," he said. "It is like the Sahara, compared with the rest of the Camargue, but I expect you know the legend of why the flat plains are covered with stones."

"No, tell me," Valda begged.

"The Crau was once believed to be the home of the Ancient Ligurians," he answered, "and the legends tell us that when Hercules was on his return from Spain he encountered them in battle. When his soldiers had exhausted their supplies of arrows and were at the mercy of the enemy, Hercules prayed to Zeus for help."

"And the god helped him?" Valda asked.

"Zeus sent a hail of stones which rained down from Heaven on the hapless Ligurians."

Roydon smiled.

"Hercules won his battle but the plains have remained a sea of stones to this day!"

They rode on through the *étangs,* the canals, the marshes, the reed-beds.

Now as they were travelling North the Camargue

became richer. There were more *taureaux* and more guardians supervising them.

The flowers were lovelier than ever and the birds rose in front of them, protesting at the intrusion into their secret wilderness.

But Valda was vividly conscious only of the joy of riding beside Roydon and at the same time savouring every moment they were together. However optimistic she tried to be, she could not help feeling afraid of what might happen when she returned home.

They had started early and by noon it was very hot and they had ridden a long way.

Now the great silver Rhône, magnificent, wide, full, and heavy, was on their right, with the barges on their way to Arles and Lyons looking like toys on the restless waters.

Across on the far bank they could see the beginning of the flat plains, with no sign of life except an occasional isolated flock of sheep.

Far in the distance, purple against the blue sky were the Alpilles mountains.

It was very beautiful and when Roydon said it was time to stop for luncheon Valda found he had chosen a place in the shade of some plane trees high above the river so that they could look across it onto the Crau.

In the pouches of their saddles *Madame* Porquier had placed various neatly done-up packages of food and a bottle of wine.

Valda opened the packets and found pasties, freshly baked bread, several different sorts of cold meats, besides the wonderful pâté which tasted quite different from any she had ever eaten before.

There was of course a multitude of different vegetables, including cold asparagus wrapped up in fresh lettuce leaves, tomatoes, aubergines, and inevitably plenty of olives.

When she had spread it all out Valda laughed.

"If we eat all this," she said, "the horses will buckle under us!"

"The expression 'as strong as a horse' was invented for those bred in the Camargue!" Roydon said. "But I agree, *Madame* is determined we shall not be hungry!"

He brought yet another package from his saddle as he spoke, which contained figs which had ripened on the side of the house and small sweet strawberries which having grown unattended had turned from cultivated plants back to being nearly wild.

They ate until Valda said she could not manage another mouthful. Meanwhile, as glasses had been forgotten, they both drank the wine from the same bottle.

"I am so happy!" Valda said as Roydon stretched himself out beside her and looked at the river glittering in the sunshine.

"I can hardly believe it is true that all this has happened so quickly," he replied.

"Yet if I feel as if I have known you all my life," Valda told him, "it is because you have always been there in my . . . heart."

"Just as you have been in mine," he said.

She slipped her hand into his.

"Will you promise me something?"

There was a serious note in her voice that he did not miss.

"What is it?"

"Promise me first!"

"I promise on one condition, that it is not something which might hurt you."

"It is something which concerns my happiness."

"Then I promise," he replied, "without reservation."

Valda's fingers tightened on his.

"That is what I wanted you to say."

"What is it you want?"

"I want you to swear by everything in which you believe . . . by everything you consider holy, that whatever the difficulties, whatever the problems that lie ahead . . . you will still . . . marry me."

The tone in her voice made him look at her sharply.

"What is making you afraid, my sweet?"

"I think I am afraid that what the gods have . . . given the gods may . . . take away."

"I promise that I intend to marry you," Roydon said.

"Whatever the difficulties?" Valda insisted.

He did not answer, and she said quickly:

"It may mean that I shall have to run away with you. Are you prepared to do that?"

"It is something which, for your own sake, I should regret your doing," he answered. "Do you really believe that your mother and Stepfather will take such an aversion to me?"

"Not to you personally," Valda answered. "It would be impossible for them to do that. But they expect me to make what they think of as a . . . suitable marriage."

"And a man without money is not suitable?"

"Only in their eyes," Valda said desperately. "You and I know money is not important. It must never be important where we are concerned. Other people do not think the same."

"I can understand their feelings," Roydon remarked. "You are very beautiful and already, although you are so young, there must be many men who wish to marry you."

"You know it is not like that in France," Valda said. "Marriage is arranged because both parties have something to offer each other."

"And what have you to offer besides your very lovely face?" Roydon asked.

Valda hesitated for a moment, then chose her words with care.

"My Stepfather belongs to an ancient family which is greatly respected."

"What is his name?"

"Merlimont."

She realised with a sense of relief that the name meant nothing to Roydon.

Her hand was still in his and he raised it to his lips, kissing her fingers one by one. Then his lips were on her palm, warm, insistent, and compelling.

She felt a little thrill go through her, and now she turned to him, her eyes pleading with him to understand.

"Promise . . . whatever he says to you . . . that you will not . . . give up. I am yours. I belong to you. Oh,

Roydon, darling . . . let us be married in Arles before I go home."

"You are not to tempt me," he answered. "But I promise, my precious, that if doing what is right fails, then we shall have to consider other ways by which we can be together."

"That is what I want to be sure you will . . . do," she said.

Roydon was still kissing her hand.

"I love you! It is going to take me all my life to tell you how much!"

"And I want to spend the . . . rest of my . . . life with . . . you."

She looked round her at the sunshine glinting on the water, the trees rustling softly overhead. Then she said passionately:

"Why can we not stay here? Why must we go back at all? No-one knows where I am. After a time they will cease looking for me and we could save so much worry and disagreeableness."

"Do you really think you would be happy living in the Camargue? Alone in the wilderness with me?"

"I can imagine nothing more wonderful! You could be a guardian and I could cook for you and we could have a little *Mas* of our own where the world would never intrude."

"You make it sound very alluring, my darling!" Roydon smiled. "But in the Winter when the winds blow in from the sea, it can be very cold and bleak."

"It would still be wild and wonderful!"

"Like you!" he answered. "But, my darling, in the future I shall be there to prevent your being wild, except of course with me!"

As he spoke he pulled her down beside him and his lips were on hers.

He kissed her gently, his lips lingering on the softness of her skin.

"I would like to keep you alone with me forever!" he said. "But I have an idea that we both have things to do in the world. Eventually perhaps some sort of service that we must give to other people. Besides, you are too beautiful to be shut up in a cage, even if it is a wilderness!"

"The Camargue could never be a cage!" Valda retorted. "It is people and houses which confine me. It is the rules of Society which make life miserable. I want to be like the wild horses, roaming at will—except of course that you must be with me!"

"We will be together!" Roydon said. "I am sure of it."

He gave a little sigh.

"If only you were older."

Valda was still.

"Do you think my Stepfather might make us wait until I am of age?"

"He might insist on a long engagement, or even perhaps a separation so that you can learn your own mind."

"I know it now. You know that I belong to you and nobody . . . nothing . . . can separate . . . us."

She spoke passionately but she knew instinctively that Roydon was still apprehensive.

Her head was against his shoulder and she looked up at him.

"You will . . . fight for me?" she asked.

"I promise you I will fight with my mind and body, my heart and soul, for what I want more than life itself!"

His words made Valda think of the Knights of Les Baux and she put her arm round his neck and drew his lips closer to hers.

"That is what I wanted you to say," she whispered.

Her lips were almost against his as she went on:

"I swear to you that whatever anyone may say or do . . . I would never marry anyone . . . else. I am yours . . . yours for all eternity!"

The words were lost against Roydon's mouth and now he kissed her with a passion that revealed the fire rising in him.

It ignited the flame within Valda too, and he kissed her until at length she made a little murmur at the wonder of it and hid her face against his neck.

Her breath was coming quickly between her lips and her heart was thumping wildly in her breast.

"I love you! I love you!" she cried. "Oh . . . Roydon . . . I love you!"

He held her very close, then he said quietly:

"We must go on, my precious. The sooner we face what lies ahead, the better it will be for both of us."

"I am so desperately . . . afraid of losing . . . you."

"You will never do that."

It was in the nature of a vow and Valda found it comforting as they packed up what was left of their luncheon. Mounting their horses, they started off again along the path that ran beside the river.

All too soon it seemed to her they were within sight of Arles, and as she looked at it in the distance it appeared dark and ominous.

Its towers and spires warned her that she was stepping from the wilderness back into civilisation and she had no idea what civilisation might mean for her!

She felt desperately that there was so much she wanted to say to Roydon, so much they had not discussed, so much that she might regret when they were not together.

"Let us stop for a little while," she pleaded. "I have a terrifying feeling that we are leaving our . . . happiness behind."

She drew in her horse as she spoke and looked back the way they had come.

"Why should we be hidebound?" she asked. "Why must we always be conventional and think of what is supposed to be right? Let us go back . . . back to the Camargue. It is there waiting for us. If we spend another month—or perhaps even a year there—when we come here again we will find things just the same as they are now."

"Would you really come back with me if I asked you to do so?" Roydon asked.

"You know that is what I want," Valda replied, and her blue eyes were very sincere under the brim of her straw hat.

"Sooner or later we would have to leave," he answered, "and do you think it would make it any easier?"

"At least we would have had that perfect time together," she said. "A time to remember."

"You are talking as if you believe we will have to separate," he said accusingly. "As if you think it inevitable that we shall be parted."

"I am praying that everything will . . . happen as we want it to," Valda said. "At the same time, I am afraid . . . of course I am afraid! What we are doing is throwing away the substance for the shadow."

Roydon did not reply and she went on:

"We are here, we are together . . . and there is no-one to . . . argue about it. If we go back now we are risking our happiness for some mistaken ideal you have about what is right and what is wrong."

Valda put out her hand to touch his arm.

"This is right as far as I am concerned," she said. "Right that I should be with you. Right that I should belong to you. Right that we should love each other. Why do we have to convince anybody else of what we know is the truth?"

He covered her hand with his own as it lay on his arm, and she felt the strength of his fingers.

"I want you for my wife," he said quietly, "and being married involves other people and the blessing of the Church."

"You were . . . prepared to . . . make love to me . . . without it," Valda said in a small voice.

"That was before I was properly aware of our love and how tremendous it is," he answered. "You bemused and beguiled me, as you well know, with your pretence of being a modern girl—of being sophisticated and experienced."

He gave a little sigh.

"I suppose all the time I knew it was untrue, and yet you were so persuasive, and at the same time so inexpressibly desirable, that I could think of nothing except that I wanted you."

"And you do not . . . want me now?"

Roydon smiled.

"You know the answer to that," he said, "but I want you in a very different way. I want you as my wife, to belong to me always! And I want you one day as the mother of my children."

He spoke very gravely and to that Valda knew she had no answer.

She looked at him and there was no need for further words. Instead he lifted her hand from his arm and kissed it very tenderly.

Then still without speaking they spurred their horses and moved on towards Arles.

The place that *Monsieur* Porquier had described to them was not far inside the town. There were shady places and little squares, and tall, narrow houses with grey shutters, until they came to a yard where other horses were stabled. There were several carriages of different styles in the centre of it.

"It is a livery-stable!" Valda exclaimed.

"And, according to *Monsieur* Porquier, the best in Arles! The owner is good to his horses and has a reputation for being a judge of them too."

A groom came out to greet them and when Roydon explained who he wanted, went in search of his master.

There was a great deal of talk, explanations as to why the horses had been brought several weeks earlier than he had expected, and finally Valda was shown ceremoniously into a small Salon with plush-covered furniture.

She was offered coffee and a glass of wine while the carriage was prepared which was to carry her on to her home.

Only when the owner of the stables had bowed himself from the room did Roydon look at the unhappiness in Valda's eyes and say gently:

"Do not be afraid, my darling. I have a feeling that your mother and Stepfather will be so glad to have you home safe and sound that they will be in a good mood to listen to what you have to tell them."

"I do not . . . want to . . . leave you."

"It will not be for long," he replied reassuringly. "My clothes are at an Hotel in the centre of the town.

As soon as I have collected them and the letters which
I suspect will have accumulated while I have been
away, I will follow you."

He paused to say:

"You have not yet told me where you live."

"The village is called St. Mert. It is very small. When
you reach it just ask for the Château."

Valda had taken off her straw hat while she drank
her coffee, and now Roydon drew her into his arms,
first touching her hair gently with his fingers, then with
his lips.

"Take care of yourself, my precious little love," he
said. "I am half-afraid that you are a mirage from one
of the *étangs* and that you have no substance in fact.
Suppose I never find you again?"

"I shall be waiting for you," Valda replied. "And
you will remember your promise? Whatever is said,
whatever obstacles are put in our way, you will marry
me?"

"I gave you my promise," Roydon answered, "and
I shall not break it."

"Then remember, if you cannot persuade my Stepfather to let us marry, I shall run away again. I shall
find you wherever you may have gone!"

She paused to say frantically:

"Give me an address where you will be in London."

"You cannot travel to London by yourself!" Roydon
protested.

"I can and I will . . . if I cannot reach you any other
way!"

"You seem so certain that your Stepfather will refuse
to listen to me."

Valda was sure that that was what he would do, but
she did not say so.

"We have to be prepared," she said evasively. "We
have to think of every detail. My father always said,
'no adventure can be successful unless one checks every
detail.' "

There was a faint smile on Roydon's face as if he
humoured a child, while he went to a desk which stood

in the corner of the room and wrote down two addresses.

"The first will find me in Paris," he said. "If in actual fact I am turned away from your Stepfather's door, I will go there and wait for at least a week. The other will always find me in London."

"I may not even be able to write to you," Valda said. "I may just appear."

"You are being very nervous about all this," Roydon said soothingly.

"I am trying to be sensible," she said. "You know as well as I do that letters can be intercepted. It has happened in history and it could happen to us."

Roydon gave her the piece of paper on which he had written the addresses.

"We must have faith, my sweet," he said. "Faith in ourselves and faith in our fate."

He did not give Valda a chance to reply. He kissed her until once again it was difficult to think of anything but him and the fire he evoked in her.

"I love you! I love you!"

Those were the last words she said to him and the words she repeated to herself as she drove away from the livery-stable in the carriage Roydon had hired for her.

She did not look back as the horses turned into the crowded street.

Someone had once told her that to do so was unlucky, and as she drove along she did not see the Churches and Palaces, the shops with their cheese and fruit, herbs, vegetables, and flowers.

All she could see was Roydon's face, and all she could hear was Roydon's voice saying he loved her.

"The gods have given . . . the gods can take away."

She could remember saying the words as if they were prophetic.

'I cannot lose him! I cannot!' she thought despairingly.

Then she remembered her fortune and knew how difficult it was going to be first to convince her Stepfather that Roydon was not interested in that, and then convince Roydon it was of no consequence.

She was concentrating intensely on what she must say when she told her mother and Stepfather about Roydon.

At the same time, she was praying with prayers that came from the very depths of her heart that they would understand. As a result, she arrived at the Château almost before she realised she had left Arles behind.

As the horses drove up the avenue of ancient trees and came to a stop outside the magnificent doorway in the centre of the great sixteenth-century building, she thought with a feeling of desperation that she was returning to prison.

The coachman drew the horses to a standstill and the footman came running down the steps to open the door. Valda entered the Hall.

The *Maître des Chambres* with an expression of stupefaction on his face hurried towards her.

"*M'mselle* Valda! You have returned!"

"Yes. I have come home."

"*Monsieur le Comte* and *Madame* are in the Salon, *M'mselle.*"

"I will go to them," Valda replied, "but listen."

The *Maître des Chambres* waited.

"A gentleman will be arriving in an hour or so. He will ask for *Mademoiselle* Burton. Bring him into the Salon immediately!"

"*Certainement, M'mselle!*" the *Maître des Chambres* replied.

He swept across the Hall, obviously so delighted to be the bringer of good news that his voice seemed to ring out as opening the door of the Salon he announced:

"*Mademoiselle* Valda, *Madame!*"

The Comte and Comtesse were at the far end of the room. They were sitting side by side on a sofa and as the *Maître des Chambres* spoke the Comtesse gave a little cry.

"Valda!"

Valda advanced towards them, conscious that she must look a little strange without a hat, her elegant Parisian habit showing signs of wear and tear from her long ride and the thorny smilax which had caught at it when they had forced their way through the thickets to photograph the wild horses.

"Valda—darling! Where have you been? How could you have done this to us?"

Valda kissed her mother and the Comtesse held her very close. There were tears in her eyes.

"We have been so worried, so distraught! How could you have gone away like that?"

"I am very sorry to have upset you, Mama. I will tell you all about it," Valda said, and turned to her Stepfather.

He was looking at her gravely and she thought with a sinking of her heart that he was not as glad to see her as her mother was.

She moved to his side and lifted her face to his.

"Forgive me, *Beau-père*."

She felt it was an effort for him to kiss her and put his arms round her.

"Please forgive me," she pleaded. "I have so much to tell you, and I am safe, as you can see."

"Your Stepfather has only just returned from Paris," her mother explained. "He has been searching for you, Valda. I cannot tell you how upset and anxious we have been."

"*Beau-père* challenged me," Valda said, "and although I did not journey to Paris without a Courier, I have been to the Camargue!"

"To the Camargue?"

Both her mother and Stepfather spoke simultaneously in sheer astonishment.

"I have brought back the most fascinating snapshots." She smiled at her Stepfather.

"You told me, *Beau-père,* that none of my talents were salable. Well, I believe I can answer that by saying that I shall be very disappointed if I have not enough photographs to hold an Exhibition."

"An Exhibition!" the Comtesse ejaculated.

"An Exhibition of photographs of wild horses and flamingos," Valda said. "You will be surprised . . . unless something has gone wrong with my camera."

"I cannot believe that you have been to the Camargue!" her mother exclaimed. "How did you get away from here? We could not imagine, if you had gone to the station, who could have taken you there."

"I travelled with the gypsies!"

"The gypsies?" The Comte's voice seemed to echo round the room.

Then almost like Roydon he said:

"How could you have taken such crazy risks? How could you have done anything so dangerous—so irresponsible—as to go off on your own like that?"

"I wanted to prove that I was capable of looking after myself," Valda replied quietly. "And also, *Beaupère,* of choosing my husband for myself."

"And you think that is what you have proved?" he asked.

"I hope you will agree that this is what I have done. The man I want to marry will be arriving to see you in an hour or so."

For a moment it seemed as if Valda had turned her mother and Stepfather into stone.

They sat completely motionless, staring at her. Then in a tone of voice by which Valda knew the Comte was keeping his temper rigidly under control, he said:

"I think you had better explain more clearly. I find this somewhat difficult to understand."

A quarter of an hour later the Comte was still repeating again and again the same words:

"It is impossible! Quite impossible! How could you credit for a moment that I would permit you to marry this man Sanford, of whom you know nothing and whom you met by chance in the Camargue?"

"I love him and he loves me," Valda said.

She had, however, a trump card to play.

It was inevitable that her Stepfather should say:

"Do you suppose for one moment that this Englishman is not aware that you are an heiress?"

Valda had deliberately not mentioned before that Roydon was not aware of her real identity.

"Because at first I thought he might know the name, as Papa was so famous," she said, "I told him my name was Burton. As far as he is concerned, I am Miss Valda Burton, a girl of no importance, and he does not even know who you are. I just told him the name was Merlimont."

"And you think he had never heard of me?" the Comte asked.

"He is English . . . why should he?" Valda retorted.

The Comte looked at his wife.

"Do you know any Sanfords?" he enquired. "Is the name well known in England?"

"I cannot remember," Valda's mother replied. "But then I have lived in France for so long."

She looked at Valda apologetically as she said:

"This young man may be very nice, my dearest, but you do understand that *Beau-père* and I cannot let you marry the first man who takes your fancy. He may in fact be a fortune-hunter!"

Valda rose to her feet.

"I have already made it very clear, Mama, that Roydon is not a fortune-hunter. He has no idea that I possess a fortune. What is more, he said quite clearly that he would never allow his wife to keep him."

"You have discussed money?" her Stepfather enquired.

There seemed to Valda no point in not telling the truth.

"Yes," she answered. "And he is not well off at the moment because his mother had a long and expensive illness."

She saw her Stepfather's lips tighten and knew exactly what he was thinking.

"I am going upstairs to change before he arrives," Valda said. "I want to make one thing quite clear. I love you both and I am deeply grateful for all the affection you have given me and the way you have looked after me. But I love Roydon in the same way that you two love each other!"

She paused to say slowly:

"We are meant for each other. I intend to marry him and nothing anyone can say will stop me!"

She saw the arguments trembling on her Stepfather's lips and went quickly from the room.

Only as she ran upstairs to her own bed-room did she realise she was trembling.

'They will try to prevent us meeting each other!' she thought.

She knew by the expression on the Comte's face that he was at his most obstinate. He would be determined, relentless. And he would never give up doing what he thought was right for her.

"I shall have to run away!" she told herself as she reached her bed-room. "It will be more difficult a second time because they are certain to take every precaution to prevent me. But somehow I will reach Roydon and we will be married before anyone can stop us!"

Her maid came hurrying to help her change, exclaiming in horror over the condition of her habit and the fact that she was wearing her red leather gypsy shoes instead of the short kid boots which had been made for her to wear riding.

Valda did not listen to what was being said.

She was hurrying to get downstairs in case Roydon should arrive before she was ready, and also thinking out plausible and persuasive arguments with which to confront her Stepfather.

She hardly noticed the very becoming gown into which her maid helped her.

It had in fact been most expensive, and only when she looked at herself in the mirror did Valda wonder if Roydon would think she was deliberately flaunting her money when he had none.

It would be bad enough for him to find that the Château was so large and impressive and that her Stepfather was *le Comte de Merlimont,* without any added contrasts to underline the position.

But it was too late to change, since she hoped at any moment to hear the sound of his wheels coming up the drive, and she ran downstairs to find, as she expected, her mother and Stepfather still in the Salon, earnestly conferring with each other.

"You certainly look better now, dearest," her mother said when she joined them. "Did you have to sleep in some vulgar and uncomfortable Inn? I cannot bear to think of it!"

"After I left the gypsies with whom I spent the first night," Valda said, and saw that her Stepfather shuddered visibly, "I stayed in a delightful *Mas*. It was so pretty, Mama, you would have loved it. There were flowers everywhere. Wisteria was growing up its walls, and climbing roses and honeysuckle scented my bedroom."

"And what were the people like?" the Comtesse enquired.

"Very charming!" Valda answered. *"Monsieur* Porquier is a *manadier* in a big way, his wife looked after me, and the food was delicious!"

"And was Mr. Sanford also staying there?" the Comtesse enquired.

"He was spending his holiday in the Camargue, as he has done before," Valda answered.

"Holiday?" the Comte enquired. "From what?"

Valda realised she had made a mistake.

Gentlemen who did not work had no reason to take a holiday. They might go on a visit, but a holiday implied that their time was not their own.

"Roydon told me he had been inspecting the vineyards of France," she explained, "and it had in fact been quite exhausting."

It sounded plausible, but she saw that her Stepfather was still suspicious.

She knew by the manner in which he squared his chin and by the look in his eyes that when Roydon arrived, his reception was not going to be a pleasant one.

Suddenly Valda was afraid.

She could feel and almost see the opposition gathering against her.

The Comte could be very formidable when he wished, and there was no use appealing to her mother, because whatever he did or said she invariably thought he was right.

Valda could feel her happiness slipping away. She had been so sure, so convinced that the wonder of her love for Roydon and his for her was something that was not of this world but a gift from the gods.

Beau-père was determined, Valda thought frantically, to make Roydon feel he was an imposter—an adventurer.

'He will make the difference between what he can offer me and what I already have seem so poignant, so ugly, that there will be nothing for him to do but go away.'

She felt a panic rising inside her. She felt she must scream out, as if her fear, like some dangerous animal, was starting to destroy her happiness.

The door opened and before the *Maître des Chambres* could speak she saw that Roydon stood there.

He appeared very different from his appearance when she had last seen him. He was now dressed in conventional dark clothes, and looked more impressive, more authoritative, and somehow even autocratic.

Valda drew in her breath.

"Mi'Lord Linslade, *Madame!*" the *Maître des Chambres* announced in stentorian tones.

* * *

Much later that evening when the stars were coming out over the high trees in the Park and the setting sun was only a faint glow in the West, Valda and Roydon walked through the long French windows and out onto the terrace.

It was actually the Comtesse who suggested it, and she gave her husband a little smile of understanding as Valda eagerly showed Roydon the way.

They walked in silence along the terrace until they stopped to lean over the balustrade, out of reach of the golden light shining from the windows of the Salon.

"Why did you not tell me?" Valda asked.

It was a question she had been longing to put to him

all through dinner, when her mother and Stepfather had toasted their happiness and she felt as if she must be in a dream.

"I had not the slightest idea it could happen," Roydon answered. "My uncle was in early middle-age and his son was only twenty-four. As it happens, I had seen neither of them for seven years!"

"But you could have told me you had such important relatives!"

"I never thought of it," he answered. "They quarrelled with my father and the possibility of my succeeding to the title never entered my mind."

He looked across the Park and added almost as if he spoke to himself:

"How could I imagine for a moment that a storm off the Isle of Wight where they were yachting would cause such a tragedy and mean the loss of two healthy lives?"

He drew in his breath as he finished:

"And also mean that I should find myself in the happy position of being able to marry without any opposition someone I love?"

"You do . . . love me?" Valda asked.

"More than I can ever tell you," he answered. "But I admit, my precious, I was extremely apprehensive when you left me and I was well aware what you were feeling."

"And yet you made me go home."

"I told you I wanted you for my wife."

"And now we can be married very soon."

"As soon as your mother and Stepfather consider it decent for me to do so, seeing that I am in mourning," Roydon answered. "And besides, I have to get the house ready for you and arrange for my aunt to move to the Dower House."

He put his arm round Valda's shoulder and drew her a little closer to him.

"It is going to be hard to wait, my precious, but it will really not be for very long."

"Even now I cannot believe that it is all going to be so easy," Valda said. "It was so lucky that Mama knew your aunt and that they were girls together when they were young."

"What did they say before I arrived?" Roydon asked.

"My Stepfather, despite the fact that you thought my name was Burton, was quite convinced you were a fortune-hunter."

"That is exactly what I am!" Roydon said. "For I cannot believe that any man could gain a more glorious, golden, valuable fortune than to be married to you. Even if you had not an exceptional talent for taking snapshots!"

He was teasing her and Valda laughed.

"You have not seen them yet! It will be so mortifying if they do not turn out."

"In which case we shall have every excuse for spending part of our honeymoon in the Camargue so that you can try again."

"Do you mean that?"

Valda's question was breathless.

"I cannot imagine anywhere else I would rather be alone with you," he answered.

"Or I with . . . you," she whispered.

"We were both looking for wild horses," he said, "and I found someone very beautiful and very wild. Someone who I want to look after and keep beside me both day and night in case she should escape me."

There was the deep note in his voice that Valda knew so well, and although it was hard to see his eyes in the darkness she knew there would be a touch of fire in them.

"I cannot help feeling . . . wild when I am with . . . you," she whispered. "You . . . excite me and your kisses . . . sweep me away from the world . . . and up to the . . . stars."

His lips were very close to hers as she spoke and now he pulled her almost roughly against him and his mouth was on hers.

Then there was that rapture, that ecstasy, that wonder which made her cling to him with a passion that equalled his own.

'I shall always be wild where he is concerned,' she thought.

She surrendered herself to the demand of his lips, feeling his arms holding her closer and still closer until it was hard to breathe.

He lifted his head and said in a voice that was triumphant:

"You are mine and there are no more obstacles, no more difficulties! We have won, my darling! We have overcome them all, and now we can be together forever!"

"For . . . ever!" Valda repeated against his lips.

She thought as she did so that her cry for love which had sent her to the Camargue had not been in vain.

She had found the answer. It was Roydon!

ABOUT THE AUTHOR

BARBARA CARTLAND, the celebrated romantic author, historian, playwright, lecturer, political speaker and television personality, has now written over 150 books. Miss Cartland has had a number of historical books published and several biographical ones, including that of her brother, Major Ronald Cartland, who was the first Member of Parliament to be killed in the War. This book had a Foreword by Sir Winston Churchill.

In private life, Barbara Cartland, who is a Dame of the Order of St. John of Jerusalem, has fought for better conditions and salaries for Midwives and nurses. As President of the Royal College of Midwives (Hertfordshire Branch), she has been invested with the first Badge of Office ever given in Great Britain, which was subscribed to by the Midwives themselves. She has also championed the cause for old people and founded the first Romany Gypsy Camp in the world.

Barbara Cartland is deeply interested in Vitamin Therapy and is President of the British National Association for Health.